Tipbook Piano

Publishing Details

This first edition published November 2001 by
The Tipbook Company bv, The Netherlands.

Distributed exclusively by the Hal Leonard Corporation,
7777 West Bluemound Road, P.O. Box 13819,
Milwaukee, Wisconsin 53213.

Typeset in Glasgow and Minion.

Printed in The Netherlands by Hentenaar Boek bv, Nieuwegein.

© 2001 THE TIPBOOK COMPANY BV

152pp.

ISBN 90-76192-36-7

Hugo Pinksterboer

Tipbook
Piano

Handy, clearly written, and up-to-date.
***The* reference manual for both beginners and advanced
pianists, including Tipcodes and a glossary.**

THE **TIPBOOK**
COMPANY

THE BEST GUIDE TO YOUR INSTRUMENT!

Thanks

For their information, their expertise, their time, and their help we'd like to thank the following musicians, teachers, technicians and other piano experts: Ted Mulcahey (Moe's Pianos, Portland, OR), Steve Sweetsir (Bucks County Piano, Levittown, PA), Albert Brussee (European Piano Teachers Association/EPTA), Carsten Dürer (*Piano News*), Louis van Dijk, Ronald Brautigam, Michiel Borstlap, Dr. Harm van der Geest, Hans Goddijn (*Pianowereld*), Henk Hupkes (Dutch Piano Technicians Association), Jan de Jong, Jakob Kamminga, Mark Kruiver, Johan Mulder, Floor Nanninga, George Olthof (Estonia Benelux), Machiel Spiering, Carin Tielen, Mariëtte Verhoeve-Hehakaya, Arnold Duin (School for Piano Technicans), Willem and Marie-José de Groot, Luuk Guinee, Bram Groothoff, Corrie de Haan, Arend Hahn, Siem Lassche (Hammond/Suzuki Europe), Hans Leeuwerik, Erik Knecht, everyone at Cristofori, Mr. Schinck, Henny Vriese, everyone at Andriessen Pianos, Marcel Riksen, and Gerard van Urk.

Anything missing?

Any omissions? Any areas that could be improved? Please go to www.tipbook.com to contact us; thanks!

Acknowledgements

Concept, design, and illustrations: Gijs Bierenbroodspot

Cover photo: René Vervloet

Translation: MdJ Copy & Translation

Editor: Robert L. Doerschuk

Proofreaders: Nancy Bishop and René de Graaff

IN BRIEF

Have you just started playing the piano? Are you thinking about buying a piano, or do you want to find out more about the instrument you already own? This book will tell you everything you need to know. There's an introduction to the instrument and to lessons and practicing, and there's information about buying, selecting, and play-testing instruments, about sizes, finishes, mechanisms, and strings, about maintenance and regulation, and why regular tuning matters, about the history and the family of the piano, and much, much more.

The best you can

Having read this Tipbook, you'll be able to get the most out of your piano, to buy the best instrument you can, and to easily grasp any other literature on the subject, from magazines to books and Internet publications.

Begin at the beginning

If you have just started playing, or haven't yet begun, pay particular attention to the first four chapters. Have you been playing any longer? Then skip ahead to Chapter 5. Please note that all prices mentioned in this book reflect only approximate street prices in US dollars.

Glossary

Most of the piano terms you'll come across in this book are briefly explained in the glossary at the end. To make life even easier, it doubles as an index.

Hugo Pinksterboer

CONTENTS

SEE WHAT YOU READ WITH TIPCODE

www.tipbook.com

In addition to the many illustrations on the following pages, Tipbooks offer you an additional way to see – and even hear – what you are reading about. The Tipcodes which you will come across regularly in this book give you access to extra pictures, short movies, soundtracks, and other additional information at www.tipbook.com.

How it works is very simple. One example: On page 6 of this book there's a paragraph about the practice pedal. Right above that paragraph it says **Tipcode PIANO-003**. Type in that code on the Tipcode page at www.tipbook.com and you will see a short movie that shows you how a practice pedal works, and what it does to the sound.

Enter code, watch movie
You enter the Tipcode beneath the movie window on the Tipcode page. In most cases, you will then see the relevant images within five to ten seconds. Tipcodes activate a short movie, soundtracks, or both, or a series of photos.

Tipcodes listed
You can find all the Tipcodes used in this book in a single list on page 130.

Quick start
The movies, photo series and soundtracks are designed so that they start quickly. If you miss something the first time, you can of course repeat them. And if it all happens too fast, use the pause button beneath the movie window.

First, make your selection: Tipcode, chords and fingering charts, or the glossary.

The Tipcode window displays movies, photo series, fingering charts, chords, and explanations of the words used in this book.

Enter a Tipcode here and click on the button. Want to see it again? Click again.

These links take you directly to other interesting sites.

Plug-ins

If the software you need to view the movies or photos is not yet installed on your computer, you'll automatically be told which software you need, and where you can download it. This kind of software (*plug-ins*) is free.

Still more at www.tipbook.com

You can find even more information at www.tipbook.com. For instance, you can look up words in the glossaries of all the Tipbooks published to date. For clarinetists, saxophonists, and flutists there are fingering charts, for drummers there are the rudiments, and for guitarists and pianists there are chord diagrams. Also included are links to some of the websites mentioned in the *Want to Know More?* section of each Tipbook.

1. A PIANIST?

Playing solo in a concert hall, at home, or in a jazz club. Accompanying a choir, a flutist, a ballet company or a musical. Playing folk music, children's songs, or pop songs. Music of today or from three hundred years ago. As a pianist, you can do it all.

Tipcode PIANO-001

As a pianist you can play an endless variety of musical styles, ranging from centuries-old classical music to the music of tomorrow, and everything in between. More music has been written for the piano than for most other instruments. This is not only because the piano has been around for so long, but also because it is a complete orchestra on its own.

Lower and higher

On a piano you can play lower notes than a double bass, and higher notes than a piccolo, the very smallest flute. You can go from note to note really smoothly, almost like a violin, or really hit the keys, making it feel like a drum set. You can play note by note, or play ten or twenty keys at once...

Accompaniment

A piano also resembles an orchestra because you can simultaneously play the melody and the accompaniment, and then you can sing along too, as many pianists do. Or you can get someone else to sing, or to play the saxophone, the clarinet, or one of the many other instruments you can play duets with.

Written on the piano

Because a piano is a complete orchestra, a lot of music is written 'on the piano' by classical composers, pop musicians, jazz pianists, cabaret artists, and numerous other musicians.

Playing by ear

On a piano, all the notes are easy to find. They're lined up side by side, from low to high. And there's a separate key for each note. That's why the piano is one of the easiest instruments to use if you want to play a tune by ear. If you need a higher sounding note, you pick a key to the right. And if you want to hear a lower pitch, simply move to the left. Only singing is easier.

Four hundred pounds plus

A piano is one of the biggest musical instruments you can buy: Even a small upright is nearly five feet wide, easily over three feet high, and weighing four hundred pounds (200 kilo) or more. There's one big advantage to that: You'll never have to take your instrument with you when you go out to a performance or a rehearsal. Which in turn has one big disadvantage: You can never be sure whether there'll be a wonderful grand piano waiting for you or an out-of-tune, tinny old upright with dicey keys.

An upright piano...

Grand

At most important concerts, whether classical, jazz, or any other style, the pianist plays a grand piano. Being a 'horizontal piano,' even the smallest grand takes up much more space than an upright or *vertical* piano – and they're more expensive too.

... and a grand.

2. A QUICK TOUR

From the outside, a piano looks like nothing more than a big cabinet with a whole lot of keys, a few pedals, and a lid. But all told, a piano consists of some ten thousand parts, most of them inside the instrument. A chapter about a piano's main components and what they do, and about the differences between upright pianos and grands.

Most pianos have eighty-eight keys. If you take a closer look at the *keyboard*, you'll see the keys are divided into alternate groups of two and three black keys. This grouping makes all the notes very easy to find.

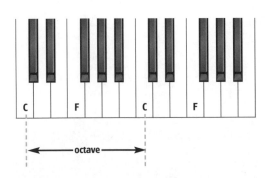

... alternate groups of two and three black keys.

The C and the F   Tipcode PIANO-002

Two examples? The white key just before *two* black keys always gives the note C. And the white key just before a group of *three* black keys gives the note F.

A little more than seven

There are always eight white keys from one C to the next. Such a group of eight is called an *octave*. A piano keyboard has a little more than seven octaves, as you can see on page 13.

Hammers and strings

Each key operates a *hammer*, inside the piano. When you press a key, the corresponding hammer strikes one or more strings. The harder you play, the harder it strikes, and the louder the sound. If you let the key go, the sound stops immediately.

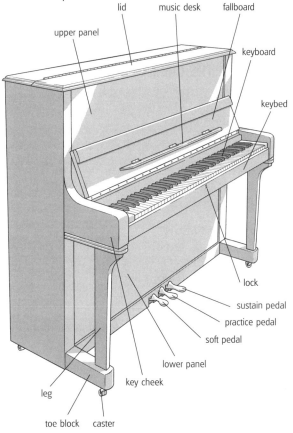

Sustain

Most pianos have three pedals. If you press down the one on the right, the sound is sustained after releasing the keys.

This explains one if its names: *sustaining pedal*. It's also known as *damper pedal* (see page 62).

Soft

On an upright, the left pedal is the *soft pedal*: it makes the instrument sound a little quieter.

Practice pedal   **Tipcode PIANO-003**

Pressing the middle pedal on many uprights moves a strip of felt between the strings and the hammers, which muffles the sound considerably. This *muffler pedal* or *practice pedal* allows you to practice without being heard in every room of the house – or the house next door. Some instruments have a lever instead of this pedal.

UPRIGHTS: THE CABINET

Most upright pianos are between 40" and 52" (100–130 cm) high. The width and the depth are pretty much the same for all instruments.

Music desk

On most uprights the *music desk* or *music shelf* is on the inside of the *fallboard*. On others it is mounted on the *upper panel* or *music panel*.

Keybed, legs, and casters

On taller pianos, the *keybed* is often supported by two legs. Most uprights with legs have wheels or *casters*, two at the back and two under the *toe blocks*.

Lid or top

When the *lid* or *top* is open, the sound becomes a little louder, brighter, and more direct.

THE BACK

At the back of an upright you will usually find a framework of several thick posts. These *posts* or *back posts* support the instrument. Behind them is a large wooden board.

Soundboard

The board behind the back posts is the *soundboard*. When

the strings vibrate, the soundboard vibrates too. This amplifies the sound of the piano – without it, you would hardly hear the instrument.

Ribs
The soundboard is reinforced by the *ribs* which run diagonally over it. The ribs are also important for the sound of the instrument.

Grip handles
The grip handles make it a little easier to move a piano. Only a little, indeed: Again, even a small upright easily weighs four hundred pounds.

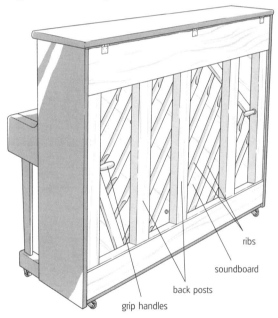

ribs

soundboard

back posts

grip handles

INSIDE
Most parts of a piano are on the inside. If you would include every spring, pin, and piece of felt, you'd count some ten thousand parts...

Action
Most of these parts belong to the *action*: the mechanism which makes the hammers strike the strings. It's looks really complicated, but the basics are easily understood.

Jack

Tipcode PIANO-004

When you press down a key, the back of that key goes up. This flicks the *jack* upwards, which makes the hammer hit the string.

Damper

As the hammer moves towards the string, the string's *damper* is removed from it. The moment you let go of the

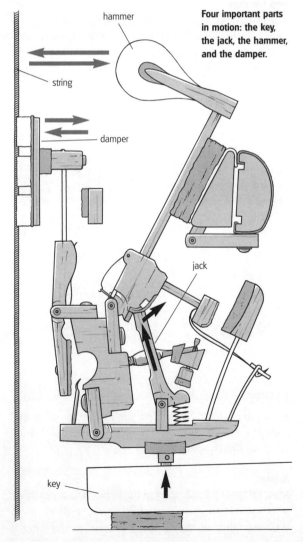

Four important parts in motion: the key, the jack, the hammer, and the damper.

hammer

string

damper

jack

key

key, the damper returns to the string. The sound stops. That's all, basically.

Ready for the next note
The hammer strikes the string only very briefly; if it would be pushed against it, the string wouldn't be able to vibrate. To enable the hammer to bounce off of the string right away, the jack springs back immediately after it has set the hammer in motion. When you let go of the key, the jack returns to its place, ready for the next note.

Long and thick, or short and thin
To produce the lowest notes, a piano has long, heavy-gauge strings, wound with copper to make them even heavier. To allow for maximum string length, these strings are stretched across the cabinet diagonally. The strings for the highest notes are short and thin.

Three strings per key
Long, heavy strings sound fuller and louder, and carry on sounding for longer than short, light-gauge strings. To prevent the low notes from sounding much fuller and louder than the high ones, the five highest octaves have three strings per key.

One or two
In the lowest bass section, each hammer strikes only one string at a time. In-between there are

One hammer, one note; three strings tuned to the same pitch.

a small number of notes which each have two identically

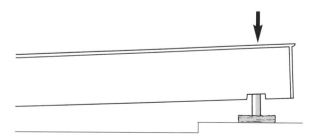

tuned strings. The sets of two and three identically tuned strings are called *unisons*.

Twenty cars

In total, a piano has around two hundred and twenty strings. Together, they exert a force of between thirty and forty thousand pounds (up to twenty thousand kilos), the weight of about twenty compact cars…

Frame

To withstand this tension, pianos have a heavy, cast-iron frame. Together with the back posts, this frame or *plate* is the backbone of the piano.

Tuning pins

The strings are tuned by turning the *tuning pins*, which are set into the *pinblock*. This sturdy piece of work, made up of several layers of wood, is usually hidden behind the frame.

Bass and treble

The strings are divided into three groups. From the top left the *bass strings* run diagonally downwards. The next

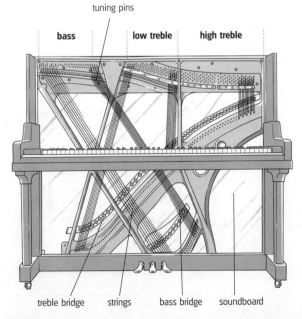

tuning pins

bass | low treble | high treble

treble bridge | strings | bass bridge | soundboard

group of strings is the *low treble* or *tenor*, and the highest octaves are called the *high treble*.

Bridges

All strings run over a *bridge*. This is a long, narrow piece of wood that transmits the vibrations of the strings to the soundboard. The bass strings have their own, fairly short bridge.

GRAND PIANOS

Grand pianos are grand, indeed. Even the smallest model takes up a lot more space than the biggest upright. The very longest grands are more than nine feet long and weigh well over a thousand pounds (500 kilos). The smallest models are half that length.

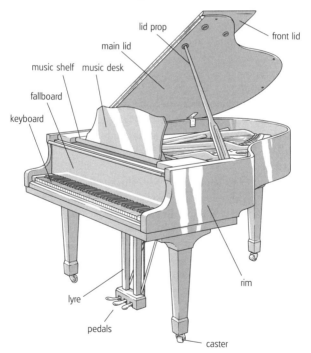

Main lid and front lid

The *lid* or *top* of a grand piano consists of two parts: the *main lid* and the *front lid*. When you open the front lid, the music desk appears.

Lid open

If you really want to appreciate the sound of a grand piano, you have to play it with the lid open. At performances, the grand piano is usually positioned so that the open lid reflects the sound toward the audience.

Strings and frame

When the lid is up, the strings and the frame can be clearly seen, as can the soundboard beneath them. Grand pianos have the same number of strings as upright pianos, the bass strings always running crosswise above the other strings: Both instruments are *cross-strung* or *over-strung*.

Action   Tipcode PIANO-005

An important difference between uprights and grands is that the hammers of a grand piano strike upwards, rather than forwards. That makes everything a little simpler in a grand, because gravity does its bit: When you let go of the keys, the dampers and the hammers fall back into place by themselves.

More control

This type of action gives you control over the sound. On a grand, it's easier to go from very soft to very loud, for example, and you can repeat notes at a higher speed.

Pedals

Most modern grand pianos have three pedals, which are attached to the *lyre*. The sustain pedal, on the right, is similar to that of an upright piano.

Una-corda pedal   Tipcode PIANO-006

The pedal on the left works differently. If you use this *una-corda pedal*, all the keys shift slightly sideways, and so do the action and the hammers. As a result, the hammers strike one less string in each unison. This not only makes the sound softer, but a little mellower too.

Sostenuto pedal   Tipcode PIANO-007

The middle pedal is the *sostenuto pedal*. If you play one or more keys and then press this pedal, only those notes will sustain when releasing the keys. All the other keys work as always: The strings are damped when you let go of the keys.

THE OCTAVES

A piano keyboard encompasses a little more than seven octaves. To avoid confusion, they have been numbered.

Middle C

The most important key to remember is the C in the middle of the keyboard. This is called *Middle C*, also known as C4: It is the fourth C on the keyboard, counting from left to right.

The A

The A to which most instruments are tuned is A4, six white keys or *naturals* to the right of C4.

C40

There are other ways to indicate the various octaves. Some count all the keys, making so middle C is C40: It's the 40th key of the keyboard. In European literature, Middle C can be indicated as c'.

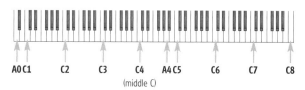

AO C1   C2   C3   C4   A4 C5   C6   C7   C8
(middle C)

Other instruments

Tipcode PIANO-008

To give you an impression of how big the piano's range really is, here's how the ranges of some other instruments compare to it. Using the Tipcode, you can hear the entire range of a piano.

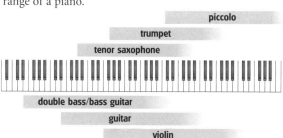

3. LEARNING TO PLAY

Is learning to play the piano difficult? No, because the keyboard makes the instrument easily accessible, and you don't need to learn to play the instrument in tune, like a violin or a clarinet. Or yes, because you are, in a way, playing two parts at the same time: one with your left hand, one with your right. A chapter about just how hard or easy it is, and about teachers, lessons, and practicing.

If you've heard a tune somewhere, it's often easier to play it by ear on a piano than on any other instrument. Why? Because one finger is enough on a piano, and because all the notes are easy to find: higher notes to the right, lower ones to the left.

All ten fingers

To really play the piano you need all your fingers, of course. You usually play the melody with your right hand, in the higher range of the keyboard, and the accompaniment

Sonatine, M. Clementi, Opus 36, No. 1 (fragment)

The upper staff shows the music for the right hand; the lower staff the music for the left hand.

with your left. Or you play two 'voices,' one with the left hand and one with the right, or really wide chords, with four or five notes per hand.

Duets
In a way, even when you're alone you are playing a 'duet' on the piano, your left hand being one musician, your right hand the other. This is one of the things that makes the piano into a 'one piece orchestra.' The only drawback is that you need to learn to read music for both hands at the same time…

Always in tune
One of the 'easy' things about a piano is that, if the instrument is properly tuned, you'll never sound out of tune: You don't have to *play* the notes in tune, as you do on a violin, a clarinet, a sax, or a trumpet. Even so, the better the pianist, the better a piano will sound – believe it or not.

LESSONS
Of course there are pianists who never met a piano teacher, but by far the majority started off with lessons – whether they play classical music or something very different.

Locating a teacher
Looking for a private teacher? Piano stores may have teachers on staff, or they can refer you to one. You can also consult your local Musicians' Union, or the band director at a high school in your vicinity. You may also check the classified ads in newspapers, in music magazines or on supermarket bulletin boards, or consult a copy of the *Yellow Pages*. Professional private teachers will usually charge between twenty and fifty dollars per hour. Some make house calls, for which you'll pay extra.

Collectives
You also may want to check whether there are any teacher collectives or music schools in your vicinity. These collectives may offer extras such as ensemble playing, master classes, and clinics, in a wide variety of styles and at various levels.

Questions, questions

On your first visit to a teacher, don't simply ask how much it costs. Here are some other questions.

- Is an **introductory lesson** included? This is a good way to find out how well you get on with the teacher, and, for that matter, with the instrument.
- Is the teacher still interested in taking you on as a student if you are doing it just **for the fun of it**, or are you expected to practice at least three hours a day?
- Do you have to make a large investment in method books right away, or is **course material provided**?
- Can you **record your lessons**, so that you can listen at home to how you sound, and once more to what's been said?
- Are you allowed to fully concentrate on **the style of music you want to play**, or will you be required to learn other styles, or will you be stimulated to do so?
- Do you have to **practice scales** for two years, or will you be pushed onto a stage as soon as possible?

READING MUSIC

If you have lessons, you'll learn to read music too. It's not really that hard; *Tipbook Music on Paper – Basic Theory* (see page 138) teaches you the basics in a handful of chapters.

Can't read

Of course there are good pianists who can't read music; they're often the ones who can play a piece of music after hearing it just once. Also, there have been countless pieces 'written' on the piano by musicians who couldn't read a note.

Why read?

If you want to play classical music, though, you need to be able to read – and being able to read has a lot of advantages for non-classical players too. If you can read, you'll have access to thousands of music books, which allows you to play new songs right away, without having heard them. It makes you more of a musician, rather than 'just' a pianist… And if you can read music, you can write it too, from your own exercises to entire compositions.

Klavar-stave

You can also put piano music onto paper without using notes, simply by indicating which keys are to be played (see example on page 72). The best-known method is Klavar or Klavarskribo. Do note, however, that there's only a limited amount of music published using this system, compared to what's available in the traditional notation.

PRACTICING

You can play piano without reading music, and without a teacher, but there's no substitute for practice.

Half an hour

How long you need to practice depends mainly on your talent and what you want to achieve. Many great musicians have spent years practicing four to eight hours a day, or even more. The more you practice, the faster you'll learn. To give you an idea: Most players make noticeable progress when practicing for half an hour a day.

Three times ten

If playing half an hour at a stretch seems too long, try dividing it up into two quarter-hour sessions, or three of ten minutes each.

Plenty of volume

A piano produces more sound than most other instruments. One of the major problems is that a lot of the piano's sound travels through walls and floors to your neighbors and the other rooms in the house. How do you keep everyone happy?

Muffle   Tipcode PIANO-003

Many upright pianos have a muffling system which makes the instrument sound a whole lot softer, but it also makes the keys feel less 'direct' (see page 63). These mufflers can be retrofitted.

Agree when to play

It's always worth talking to your neighbors and housemates to agree set practice times. This often works well and costs nothing.

Walls and floors

You can take steps to reduce the amount of sound traveling through walls and floors. If you have a concrete floor, it can help if you put the instrument on special *caster cups* (see pages 86–87) or other sound-absorbing material. There is little point in placing muffling materials between the piano and the wall, as this mainly makes the instrument sound dull while hardly reducing the loudness. Insulating the entire room is another option. First, read one of the books available on the subject, or consult a specialized contractor.

Headphones

Any piano can be provided with a system that allows you to play the instrument using headphones, so no one hears you play at all. These systems include a rail that stops the hammers right before they hit the strings. The sound you hear through your headphones comes from a *sound module*, mounted under the keybed.

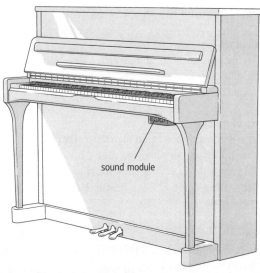

sound module

A piano with a basic sound module.

Digital piano

Rather than buy or retrofit a piano with such a system, you can get yourself a digital piano – instead of or in addition to a regular one. A digital piano has no strings, but uses *samples* (digital recordings), just like a sound module.

Though the good ones sound real close to regular 'acoustic' instruments, they're still different. One major point is that the sound comes from speakers, rather than from a wooden soundboard. The action is slightly different too. There's more about digital pianos and pianos with sound modules in Chapter 7.

CDS, COMPUTERS, AND MORE

Next to the many piano books available, you can use all kinds of different media for practicing too. For instance, there are CDs on which the piano part has been left out. So you can play with a full orchestra, or with another pianist, or play a duet with a violinist, without actually having to get real musicians to join you.

Computerized lessons

As you can read in Chapter 7, digital pianos and sound modules can be hooked up to a computer, which can be turned into a private teacher by using the right software. You can also use your computer for practice without hooking it up to your piano. For instance, there are programs which can slow down difficult phrases without changing the pitch, so you can find out how they were played note by note. Other programs teach you how to read, or simulate a complete band or orchestra for you to play along with – and there's much more.

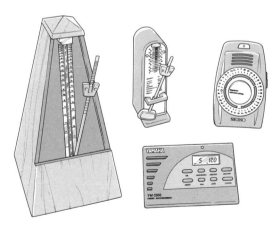

Two mechanical (clockwork) and two electronic metronomes.

Video lessons

There are video lessons too, most of them aimed at styles other than classical music, be it jazz, blues, rock, or some other style.

Metronome

As a pianist you have to be able to keep time, just like every other musician. That's why its good to practice with a metronome now and again. This is a device which produces bleeps or ticks, so you can tell right away when you're speeding up or slowing down. Sound modules often have a built-in metronome.

Listen and play

And finally, visit festivals, concerts, and sessions. Watch and listen to soloists, orchestras, or jazz groups. One of the best ways to learn to play is seeing other musicians at work. Living legends or local amateurs – every concert's a learning experience. The best way to learn to play? Play a lot!

4. BUYING OR RENTING?

Even the cheapest new pianos cost some fifteen hundred dollars or more. On the other hand, a good piano will last for decades, and it keeps its value well. If it's still too much money to spend all at once, or if you first want to try an instrument out for a while, you can rent one. A chapter about piano prices, about buying, renting, and leasing, buying new or secondhand, and about piano stores. In Chapter 5, *A Good Piano*, you'll learn about what to pay attention to once you're in the store.

Considering the huge cabinet and the thousands of parts of the action, fifteen hundred dollars isn't all that much money for a new upright piano – yet the cheapest instruments are available from that price. You'll pay around ten times as much for the most expensive.

Grand pianos
Grand pianos cost more indeed. They start around seven or eight thousand, and again you'll easily pay ten times as much for the most expensive models.

Long-lasting
Because they last a long time, good pianos have a high trade-in value. If you exchange your instrument for a more expensive one, you may even get back what you originally paid for it – or just a little less.

A decent piano
If you are looking for a new upright piano which isn't too expensive but sounds good, plays well, stays in tune, and will

probably last at least ten years without major problems, expect to pay three to four thousand dollars or more. If you want to pay less, you can't set your sights as high.

A richer tone

The difference between expensive and cheap pianos is not easy to see. What are you actually paying for if you spend more money? In the first place for a better tone, of course. More money buys you a 'richer' sound.

Taller is bigger

When comparing uprights within one quality range, more money will often buy you a taller instrument – the taller an upright is, the 'bigger' it can sound. Do note, however, that there are great-sounding small uprights – and four-foot ones that don't sound any good at all.

Better materials

When building more expensive pianos, more of the work is often done by hand, and more expensive materials are used. That may mean better wood, which has been dried for years so that it won't shrink or expand anymore; better felt for the hammer heads and the dampers; better strings; a finish that has been applied with more care and in more coats to last longer; and much more – all things which can make an instrument sound better and more enjoyable to play, and which make it last and hold its value for longer.

More work

A new piano that costs more will – usually – have had more work done on it. For instance, a good piano may have been tuned up to ten times before it leaves the factory.

Bad pianos

Is there such as thing as a bad piano? Yes. A piano which goes out of tune quickly, for instance, or a piano made from wood which has not been properly dried and cured, so that keys, panels, and other parts may warp. Unfortunately, these are all things you are unlikely to be able to see when the instrument is brand new. A few tips: Read up a lot and ask plenty of advice before you buy; go to several stores and always ask what is and what is not covered by the warranty (see pages 26–27).

Upright or grand?

Money and space provided, many pianists will go for a grand piano. After all, the upright was invented only because grands take up so much room. So is a grand always better? Not necessarily, and certainly not if you're talking about instruments of roughly the same price. After all, an upright piano of ten thousand dollars will usually be of a higher quality than a grand with a similar price tag.

The other one

When in doubt between the two, some prefer the feel, the sound, or possibly the looks of a small, affordable grand, while others go for the upright, because it sounds or plays better, or takes up less space… And there are lots of pianists who went out to buy a grand and came home with an upright – or the other way around.

SECONDHAND

Secondhand instruments can be bought privately, through classified ads or via family or friends, or from a piano store or a piano tuner. Prices range from next to nothing – usually for pianos that haven't been played or tuned for years – to thousands of dollars. Expect to pay about a thousand dollars or more for an upright that you'll enjoy playing for a number of years without expensive repairs.

Appraisal

If you're buying a piano from a private party, have it appraised before you buy, even if it's a cheap instrument: If a four hundred dollar piano really needs a lot of work, it can easily cost a thousand dollars to make it playable. Judging a piano on its technical merits, rather than its sound or its feel, is something that should be left to a piano tuner or technician. A written appraisal usually costs between seventy-five and a hundred and fifty dollars. The report may also tell you what needs to be done to the instrument, and what it'll cost.

In the store

Rather than buy privately, you might look for used instruments in piano stores. This may be a bit more expensive, but it has a lot of advantages. First, the instruments will usually be inspected, tuned, voiced, and regulated. You can choose from a number of instruments, and you're able to compare them. You can come back if you have questions or if problems crop up. Also, you can be confident that you're not paying more than the instrument is worth. What's more, the instrument will usually come with a warranty. Some warranty certificates even show which parts, if any, have been replaced or reconditioned. Technical buying tips for secondhand instruments are on page 66.

RENTING A PIANO

Many piano stores rent out instruments too. Rental fees start as low as twenty-five dollars a month. The monthly fee is often one or two percent of the retail price. So, for a five-thousand-dollar piano, you'll be paying between fifty and a hundred dollars per month.

Tuning, delivery, insurance

The rental fee also depends on what is included. A few examples: Are maintenance and tuning included (most pianos need to be tuned two or three times a year), are delivery, insurance, and a bench included? Will you get a new or a used instrument? One more question: Is there a minimum rental period? Some stores start with six months; at other stores you can rent a piano per month.

Minus the rental fee

If you eventually decide to buy the instrument, a part or all of the rental payments can often be applied to the purchase price of the piano, or to the price of a similar or more expensive instrument. How much will be applied often depends on how long you have rented the instrument. There's a wide and pretty confusing variety of rent and rent-to-own programs, so always read the agreement carefully before you sign it, and compare the programs of various stores.

THE STORE

The more instruments a store has on display, the harder it can be to choose one. That said, the more instruments there are to choose from, the better the chance that you'll find exactly what you're looking for… It's especially important that you are given the time and space to play the instruments, preferably more than once, and that the staff is knowledgeable and enjoying their work – and in a good store, you'll often find that they can play the instrument too.

Sound advice

Good information is crucial when it comes to pianos, because it's not easy to spot the differences between them, and because these are expensive instruments, which you want to last you for years. Good information is also important because pianos may only show their true quality after months, or even years.

Discuss

This book offers a good deal of the information you need, but without good advice in the store, choosing an instrument remains difficult. A good salesperson can help you to come to a good choice by discussing things like the type of music you play, how long you've been playing, the piano you're used to and the room where the instrument will be placed – rather than simply telling which piano you should choose.

Tuned and ready to play

In a good store, all the instruments will be tuned and ready to play. You shouldn't buy a piano that hasn't been tuned, if only because you can't hear its true sound. What about a piano that doesn't play well? The problem may simply be poor regulation. If you are thinking of buying it you should definitely wait until the instrument has been regulated before you choose – and be sure to try it again first.

Go back

Most piano stores won't mind if you come back a few times. Most likely you'll need to, in order to make your best choice. Many buyers will visit a number of different stores over a period of a week or so. Not only to compare the instruments by different makes, but also the stories that go with them. Have you fallen in love with a piano at first sight? That's often a good sign. Still, it's no bad idea to come back the next day to listen to it once more.

Try out

Pianos hardly ever sound the same in the store as in your home. It's possible, though unlikely, that when the piano is finally delivered to your home you will be disappointed by its tone. Some stores will even allow you to exchange the instrument, and there are even some stores that will let you try the instrument out at home. Of course, you'll have to meet delivery costs yourself (see pages 98–99). Other stores have try-before-you-buy rental programs for a day, a week or a month.

The same one

No two pianos sound exactly the same, even if they're 'identical' instruments. So always make sure you get the piano you selected in the store, and not the 'same' one from their warehouse. To be on the safe side, you can ask to have the serial number of the instrument noted on your receipt.

Another piano

Some stores apply the full price you paid for the piano you bought there toward the price of another piano, provided you come to buy one within a certain period of time, say one or two years. Usually, the new piano should have the same or a higher retail price than the first one. Again, ask for the exact conditions before you buy.

Warranty

Carefully study what is and what's not covered by the instrument's warranty. For example, it should cover both parts and labor: it may costs hundreds of dollars to replace a relatively cheap part. A long term warranty (fifteen, twenty years, or even more) sounds attractive, but may not add a lot to your investment: Usually, defects that are covered by the warranty will emerge within the first years. Most companies offer a five to ten-year warranty.

Tips

Please note that warranties are often valid only if the instrument is sold by an official dealer. Another important aspect is whether the warranty is transferable to another owner, should you decide to sell the instrument. Final tip, encompassing everything else: Study the warranty agreement, and compare warranties from store to store and company to company. Good pianos are always backed by a solid factory warranty. Distributors and stores may offer additional warranty.

Financing

Some stores offer financing possibilities. Always compare the conditions with those offered by your bank.

FINALLY

A piano is one of the few instruments that you don't tune yourself. In most cases, the instrument needs to be tuned twice or three times a year. Including the required additional maintenance, this will usually cost some two to three hundred dollars per year.

Take someone along

When you go looking for a new instrument, take along another piano player – especially, but not only, if you don't yet play yourself. A second player will allow you to listen together and discuss, and there are other advantages besides: See Chapter 6, *Play-testing*.

More, more

If you want to make an informed purchase, stock up on piano magazines, and on all the brochures and catalogs you can find. Besides containing a wealth of information, the latter are designed to make you want to spend more than you have, or have in mind – so ask for a price list too. The Internet is another good source for up-to-date product information. And of course there are many more piano books as well. You can find more about these resources beginning on page 131.

Fairs and conventions

One last tip: If a music trade show or convention is being held in your area, check it out. Besides lots of instruments you can try out and compare, you will also come across plenty of product specialists, as well as numerous fellow pianists who are always a good source of information and inspiration.

5. A GOOD PIANO

Choosing a piano becomes easier if you know more about the instrument. This chapter focuses on all tangible and visible aspects of the instrument, and how they may influence its performance: from the dimensions and the cabinet to the action, the pedals, and the strings, including tips for judging used instruments. Chapter 6 concentrates on what to listen for when choosing a piano.

Just about all the parts of a piano contribute to the tone of the instrument, from the back posts to the strings, and from the soundboard to the dampers. What makes a piano different from most other instruments is that you can't simply replace any of its parts and expect to influence the tone as easily as saxophonists can experiment with different mouthpieces and reeds, or violinists with strings and bows.

Voicing
However, it is possible to have the tone of a piano adjusted or improved, for instance by making the hammers softer or harder (*voicing*), and of course you can have the strings or the hammers replaced – but that's basically only done when they're worn out. Mind you, these are all jobs for a professional. There's more on this in Chapter 10.

The sum of the parts
In a piano, the tone is the sum of all the parts. No one instrument is ever better than another just because a better type of wood has been used. What matters more is whether that type of wood suits that particular instrument.

DIMENSIONS

The height of an upright piano is a very important dimension. The very smallest uprights are about three feet high (90 cm), and the tallest about a foot or more higher (120–130 cm), although occasionally you may see even taller ones. A taller instrument has a bigger soundboard and longer strings, which together produce a 'bigger,' more resonant sound and more volume. It's the same with grand pianos, and that's why most concert halls have a grand piano around 9' long.

Louder, but just as soft

It's quite easy to hear the difference between a smaller and a taller upright of the same quality. The tall one has a richer, fuller, more powerful and resonant tone and, if you play with more force, more volume – yet it can sound just as soft as the smaller model. The difference is usually strongest in the lower octaves.

Different feel

A tall piano will also feel different to play than a real small one: the lower the piano, the more the action has to be adapted to fit the reduced dimensions (see pages 45–46).

Size isn't everything

Of course, the quality of an instrument is more important than its height alone. An expensive 48" (120 cm) piano can easily sound 'bigger' and richer than a taller but much cheaper instrument. What if you have to choose between two models of the same price, one a little taller and the other a little smaller? Then just buy the piano that sounds the best and that you feel most comfortable playing. Size isn't everything.

How much more

How much you pay for a few extra inches – and tone – depends, among other things, on the make and the price range. If, for instance, you pay around three thousand dollars for a 43" (110 cm) instrument, then a 47" may cost you a thousand dollars extra from one make, and more than twice that amount extra from another. Why? Perhaps because the second manufacturer installs a better action in the taller model, and the first one does not.

Two tips

In most cases, you'll barely hear a difference of two inches. Another tip: some taller instruments simply have an extra tall cabinet. Of course, they don't sound any bigger than a piano with a smaller cabinet but a soundboard which is the same size.

Spinet, console, or full-size

The shortest upright pianos are called *spinets* (up to some 40" or 100 cm high); the tallest models, known as *full-size uprights*, are usually between 48" and 52" (120–135 cm). In-between are *console* and *studio* pianos.

No standard sizes

There are no standard sizes for these types. For instance, some say that studio pianos range from 43" to 47", others use the same name for pianos of 49" and upwards. You may also come across different names, like *consolette*, which is a small console.

Space

A tall piano looks much bigger than a small one. Even so, both usually take up the same amount of floor space. Most pianos are between 22" (55 cm) and 24" (60 cm) deep, and the differences in width are very minor too.

Grand or upright?

Does a grand piano always sound 'bigger' than an upright? No. It often seems that way, partially because grands are usually played with the lid open, and uprights with the lid closed. What about the size of the soundboard? The soundboard of a 5.5' grand piano (175 cm) is often about the same size as that of a 50" (130 cm) upright, so you would only expect to hear the difference from grand pianos that are longer than that.

Choosing

Having said that, there are other differences to take into account. An important one is that the sound of a grand piano – with its lid open – can spread out freely in all directions from the soundboard, which is much less the case with an upright, the soundboard usually being close to the wall. Many pianists feel much more 'inside the sound' when they play a grand piano. And yet pianists sometimes opt for an upright when they were looking for a grand… So, if you have the money and the space for either, it comes down to playing, listening, and comparing.

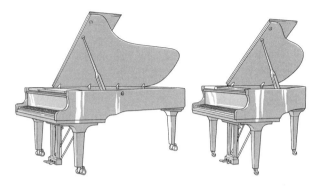

A 9' (275 cm) concert grand piano and a 5' (150 cm) baby grand.

Grand piano names
The smallest grand pianos are often referred to as *baby grands*. They usually are from 4'6" to 5'6" (135–165 cm). The longest models, called *concert grands*, are usually about nine feet (275 cm), and a few companies produce even longer ones. In-between sizes are known as *medium grands* or *small concert grands*.

The difference
In a concert grand, the soundboard is nearly twice as big as in a baby grand, and the longest string is about twice as long – and you can most certainly hear that difference.

More feet, more dollars
If you go from a 5'6" foot grand to a similar instrument one foot longer, it'll easily cost two or three thousand dollars more. When it comes to the very best instruments, the price difference is likely to be two or more times as big.

THE OUTSIDE
Uprights and grand pianos come in a wide variety of styles and finishes, from high-gloss black to wood finishes in many different colors, and from very basic designs with controlled lines to impressively-carved rococo models.

High-gloss black

High-gloss instruments are treated with a thick coat of polyester or finished with traditional or polyurethane (synthetic) lacquer. The glossy high-polish polyester coating, as used by most European and Asian makers, is pretty tough, small scratches are quite easily removable, and it shines easily. Traditional lacquer requires more care. Black is the most popular color for high-gloss instruments, followed – at a large distance – by white.

Silk-gloss or satin

The advantage of silk-gloss or satin instruments is that they don't show up dust, fingerprints, and other grime as clearly.

Transparent

The same goes for transparent finishes, high-gloss or satin, that allow you to see the veneer – the thin ply of wood used on the outside of the instrument. Common types of veneer include oak, mahogany, cherry, and walnut, and often several types are combined. Each type of wood has its own hue and pattern.

Unfilled

On some instruments you can more than just see the wood, you can feel it too: The grain has not been filled.

Wax

There are also matte-finish instruments available in which the wood is protected using wax instead of lacquer.

Synthetic outer ply

Cheap upright pianos can be finished with a synthetic outer ply rather than wood. This makes the instrument cheaper to make and easier to maintain.

French polish

French-polished instruments are finished with shellac, a natural (usually black) finish with a warm, silky sheen. This type of finish is most common on older instruments, although there are makes that still offer new French-polished pianos. Shellac is both more vulnerable and more expensive than polyester or lacquer (see also page 89).

Custom designs

Some manufacturers offer pianos in custom colors and designs, the only problem being that you can't play the instrument before you decide to buy it. Some piano stores may finish pianos themselves: You first choose an instrument and then have it finished in your favorite color or design.

Inside

The panels are almost always finished on the inside too. This protects the wood and reduces the chances of warping.

More expensive or not

With one make, a high-gloss finish is more expensive than a satin finish; with the next make it's the other way around. Sometimes it depends on the type of wood used to finish the instrument – cherry costs more than oak, for example. There's almost always an additional charge for special colors and finishes.

Details

There are manufacturers who make their instruments more attractive with details such as walnut strips around the edges, upper panels with inlaid ovals or decorated with

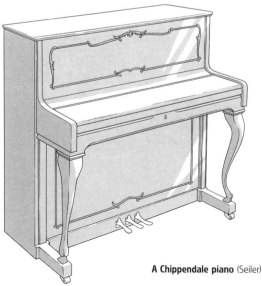

A Chippendale piano (Seiler)

Rococo grand (Blüthner).

Modern piano (Sauter).

figures, chrome-finish instead of gold-colored (brass) pedals, hinges, and locks or – especially on grands – special wood types on the inside of the cabinet. Bird's-eye maple, a highly figured type of wood, is a well-known example.

Matching your interior

Many manufacturers also produce instruments to match interiors in a particular style – Chippendale uprights, for instance, with artfully twisted legs and other ornate features, or heavily decorated rococo-style grands. At the other end of the scale, there are instruments designed for uncluttered modern interiors. Some manufacturers offer a choice of three, four or more styles for each series of pianos, such as Queen Anne, Country Classic (American Colonial design), and Italian or French Provençal.

Decorations

Apart from the color and the height, pianos may have many other small differences that you'll notice only if you know where to look. A few examples: The corners of the keybed may be rounded or angular; the edges of the lids may be sawn straight, or they may be curved; the legs may be round, square or double, they may be fluted or not, and they may run straight down or tapered toward the bottom…

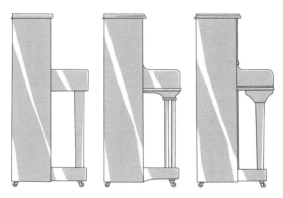

... if you know where to look...

With or without legs

There are three basic styles of cabinetry for uprights: without legs, with free-standing legs, and with legs and toe blocks. The latter type is often a taller piano, referred to as *institutional* or *professional*. Smaller pianos without legs are known as *continental* instruments, the smallest ones often having an upper panel that's slanted backwards. The third type usually features a decorated cabinet and legs, hence the name *decorator style*.

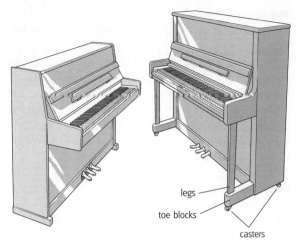

legs

toe blocks

casters

On small continental models, the upper panel is often slanted slightly backwards.

Casters and wheels

Casters make an upright a little easier to shift around a room, but you shouldn't really use them to move it any distance – especially if the instrument has free-standing legs. If a piano needs to be moved regularly, from one room to another, or within one room, you need bigger wheels. Such wheels are fitted to *school pianos* (see the

Decorator with free-standing legs.

illustration on page 128), which also have other extras like protective brackets, a lock for the lid, and sometimes a wooden plate to protect the soundboard. Grand piano casters come in various sizes, some featuring a brake. Special sets of wheels that make moving a grand piano even easier are also available.

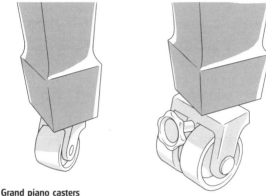

**Grand piano casters
in various sizes, with and without a brake.**

Higher keyboard, higher seat

Fitting casters or larger wheels to a piano will raise the keyboard, which possibly means you may want your seat to be a little higher (see pages 84–85). A different piano may require a different seat height too: the height of the white keys varies between 26" and 28" (66–72 cm), and that's more than it looks on paper. If the keyboard is too low for you, the piano can be put on special caster cups (see pages 86–87). Do watch out that the pedals don't end up too high.

Mind your knees

If you have long legs, pay attention to the height of the bottom of the keybed, which usually ranges from about 24" to 28" (60–70 cm).

LIDS, CABINETS, AND BACK POSTS

The large panels and posts of a piano are not the most important components when you are choosing an instrument, but there are a few things that are worth knowing about them.

Fallboard

On most upright pianos, the fallboard or *fall* consists of two hinged parts. That's easier to make than a curved, one-piece fallboard. On some instruments the fallboard is provided with a system that prevents it from slamming shut, often bearing a name like *soft-fall*, *soft-close*, or *slow-close fallboard*.

Pads

To prevent damaging the finish, uprights may have two small rubber pads which catch the fallboard when you open it. Just to be on the safe side, always check that the fallboard easily opens and closes without rubbing at the sides.

Locking the fallboard

If the fallboard doesn't have a built-in lock, you can buy a U-shaped lock which fits around it. There are also built-in and retrofit locks that lock the fallboard from the side.

Music desk

On most uprights the music desk is usually 24" to 34" (60–80 cm) wide. The wider models can hold four sheets side by side. To stop the music from sliding off, music desks often have ridges or a raised edge, or they are lined with felt, leather or vinyl. If the music desk is attached to the upper panel, rather than on the inside of the fallboard, the music stays put when you close the instrument. These desks may extend almost the whole width of the instrument.

Lid

To make the sound of an upright piano a little more direct, you can open the lid. On some pianos, only the front half of the lid opens, so you can leave any objects on top of the back half. Other lids are hinged at the back, and still others (known as *grand-style lids*) are hinged at the side, or in the middle of the lid, so you can open either the left- or the right-hand half.

More volume

To get a little more volume – for instance if they want to play with a drummer – pianists sometimes take off the entire upper panel. That's easily done and doesn't require

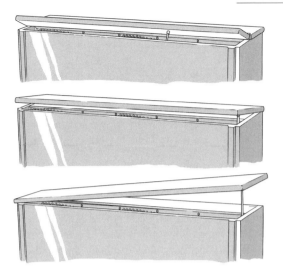

Different lids: a hinge in the middle, at the back and at the side.

any tools. Please note that there is a risk that the backs of the hammers will now hit the fallboard. This is not a problem in itself, as you can easily remove the fallboard too. However, that does mean losing your music desk and exposing the vulnerable action parts to possible damage.

Openings
Some pianos have special openings to make the tone a bit fuller or more direct. These might be at the back – just under the lid, for instance. Other instruments have part of the upper panel made of cloth, or a kind of grillwork set into the lower panel.

Grand pianos: the front-lid
Many grand pianos have some small rubber pads glued onto the front lid. These pads prevent the front lid from touching the main lid when you open it. They are always visible when the front lid is closed, and it's barely possible to remove them without damaging the lacquer. Instead of these pads, you can use a (removable) cushion for the same purpose.

The music desk
The music desk of a grand piano can often be set in three or four different positions. The music shelf, to which it is

attached with hinges, can be slid out of the instrument completely to provide access to the tuning pins. Pianists who don't use sheet music sometimes remove the music shelf permanently, which slightly opens up the sound.

You can go the other way too: If you want a grand to produce as little volume as possible, but still want to use the music desk, then remove the music shelf, then close the front lid and place the shelf with the music desk on top of it.

Main lid

The main lid of a grand can usually be opened in two settings. Occasionally the *lid prop* or *top stick*, which holds it up, allows for three settings: In the lowest one, the lid is only slightly open. Some grands have a big round knob on the side. This operates a hook that holds the grand's lid in place during (vertical) transportation.

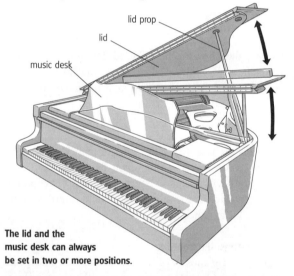

The lid and the music desk can always be set in two or more positions.

Upright: the back posts

At the back of an upright there are often three to six thick back posts that give the instrument extra solidity. The required number of posts and their thickness and location depends mainly on the construction of the rest of the instrument. Some smaller uprights don't have back posts at all. In this case, a heavier frame is used. Building an instrument without back posts is cheaper, and makes the cabinet around two to four inches (5–10 cm) less deep.

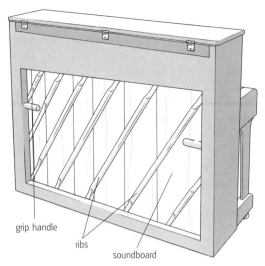

grip handle

ribs

soundboard

A piano without back posts:
The thick vertical posts are missing (see page 7).

Grand piano: braces

The 'back posts' on grand pianos are referred to as *braces*, and they come in all kinds of variations – the *tone collector*, for instance, in which the posts come together at one point. Of course, while it can certainly affect the tone, you shouldn't choose or reject a particular instrument just because of the arrangement of the back posts, nor for the number of posts or the exact dimensions of other components large or small.

Spruce or beech

The type of wood used for the back posts is another subject that has been much discussed. For instance, some experts say posts made of solid spruce make the tone a little warmer, whereas mahogany supposedly helps produce a slightly stronger tone. In the end, the type of wood chosen was the one the manufacturer felt suited his instrument the best, whether for reasons of tone, price, or strength, or all three.

Upright cabinet

The panels, lid, and fallboard of an upright piano are often made from laminated wood, usually composed of plies of poplar or birch. On cheaper models, particle board (chipboard, flake board) is sometimes used, or MDF

(Multi-Density Fiberboard), a very heavy material made of very fine wood fibers. It's often impossible to tell exactly which material has been used, not least because the outer plies and edges are often made of 'real' wood, even if the rest isn't.

Moisture

Some of these wood-based panels are more resistant to warping than solid wood panels. This may be worth taking into account if you are intending to put the piano somewhere where temperature and humidity vary a lot. The drawback with particle board is that it is less sturdy, and screws can come loose rather easily.

Rim

Depending on the design of the instrument, the cabinet (of an upright) itself or the *rim* (of a grand piano) may influence the tone too. Maple or beech are often used for grand piano rims, and a few makes have rims made of spruce, the same material used for the soundboard.

THE KEYBOARD

Most uprights and grand pianos have eighty-eight keys. Older models sometimes have three fewer at the high end, while an occasional, expensive long grand has four or even nine extra keys in the bass register. The extra long strings which go with those keys also contribute to the tone of the entire instrument.

Ivory or synthetic

In the past, the white keys were almost always covered with ivory. The synthetic *key covering* which is now mostly used feels a little smoother (more slippery, some would say), but it discolors less quickly and it's easier to maintain. Some brands have synthetic imitation ivory with names like *ivoplast* or *ivorite*. Other manufacturers cover the keys of particular models with bone or mammoth ivory, from mammoths which have been buried under the Siberian ice for thousands of years.

Ebony or plastic

The black keys or *sharps* are often made of plastic. Only

more expensive models and older instruments still have wooden sharps, usually made of ebony. Many pianists prefer wood to plastics because they say it feels better, again, being less slippery.

Balanced

In order to balance out the keys, small pieces of *key lead* are set into them. In uprights they are often placed near the far ends of the keys, where they are invisible from the outside. If they are set into the side of the keys, as in grand pianos, you can sometimes just about see them if you press down the neighboring keys completely.

Key dip

In a well-regulated grand piano, the keys can be pressed down about 0.4" (1 cm). If this depth or *key dip* is too big, it takes too long before the instrument responds, which makes it harder to play fast. If the key dip is too small, the dynamic range (the difference between loud and soft) will be reduced. Of course, the key dip has to be the same for each key, regulated to the nearest hundredth of an inch.

Equally high, evenly spaced

On used instruments especially, it's a good idea to check whether all the keys are at the same height (usually a matter of proper regulation) and whether the spaces between keys are equally wide all the way along the keyboard. The keys must not touch each other at any point.

Long keys, short keys

The keys of a grand piano are slightly longer than those of an upright, which is one of the reasons why a grand plays differently. Very short keys, such as the ones on some small pianos, do not play very easily. The action, which has been adapted to fit the smaller cabinet, plays a role too.

Keyboards

Rather than make all their own components, most piano manufacturers buy them at specialized factories. Kluge and Langer, for instance, are two well-known keyboard makers. Some piano manufacturers buy all their keyboards from these companies; others use them only for their top models.

Is better-known better?

A tip: Most manufacturers won't use expensive parts by famous makes in a piano that isn't really worth it. On the other hand, a list of prestigious brand names doesn't necessarily mean a piano will sound or play great.

THE ACTION

When you press down a key and let go of it again, you set a whole series of parts in motion. This mechanism, the action, works well only if it's properly regulated – and there are twenty-five or more points of adjustment per key...

Seventy parts

Each key controls an action made up of some sixty or seventy parts, from the *front-rail pin* to the *damper-spring bushing* and the *whippen-flange screw*. Exactly what all of those minor parts do has been described extensively in countless technical piano books.

Simultaneously

The action is as complicated as it is because many things have to happen simultaneously or in quick succession: hammer to string, damper off, hammer straight back and ready for the next note, damper back...

Quality

An instrument with a better action plays better, feels better, and lasts longer. Of course, even the best action won't feel good if it isn't properly regulated.

Let-off   Tipcode PIANO-009

One example of a point of adjustment is the *let-off*. If you look inside a piano while very slowly pressing down a key, you'll see that the hammer falls back just before it touches the string. The *let-off*, also known as *set-off* or *escapement*, is adjusted via the *let-off button*. This button controls when the jack escapes from under the hammer butt, so that the hammer can fall back.

Too soon, too late

If the hammer falls back too soon, you won't hear a thing at all if you play very softly, playing loudly becomes difficult, and even producing a decent-sounding note is tricky. If the adjustment is off in the other direction, the hammer may hit the string twice when you play softly.

Type of action

Smaller upright pianos have different actions, adapted to fit the smaller case. As a result, they may have a different

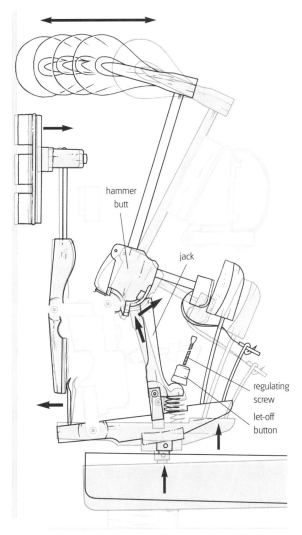

hammer
butt

jack

regulating
screw

let-off
button

The let-off: the let-off button controls when the jack escapes from under the hammer butt, so that the hammer can fall back.

'feel' than taller pianos. This difference is largest when you compare a spinet to a full-size upright. Spinets and some other small pianos have an *indirect-blow action* or *drop action*: The action is mounted below the keys. Taller uprights have a *direct-blow action*. All the same, an expensive small piano will still play (and sound) better than a cheap tall one.

Not all the same

Every instrument 'feels' different, regardless of its size. Some have a light touch; others will feel a bit heavier, requiring more power. This mainly reflects the force with which you need to press the keys down and the force they come back up with (the *up weight*). A good ratio between the two is important for the repetition speed of the keys.

Touch weight

If you like a solid-feeling keyboard, you're probably more likely to choose an instrument with a fairly high *touch weight*. The touch weight is a combination of the up weight and the *down weight* (the force required to play a soft note).

Figures

The down weight usually varies between 1.6 and 1.95 ounces (45–55 grams) and the up weight between 0.7 and 1.05 ounces (20–30 grams). Of course, playing the instrument will tell you a lot more about it than these numbers ever will. Some brochures mention the figures anyway; most don't.

Lighter or heavier

A piano that plays quite heavily can be adjusted to feel a bit lighter, and vice versa.

Further up the key

Usually, you can best tell how heavy or light the piano feels by playing fast passages. You may also try to feel the difference by playing with your fingers further towards the back of the keys. Some chords automatically force you to do that.

Even

All keys must feel the same. Play fast and slow phrases, play

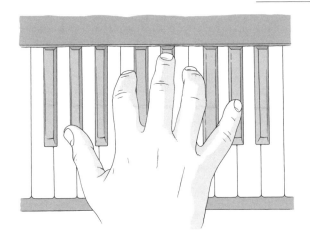

An A-flat major chord: You feel the difference better further up the key.

loudly and softly, and use the entire keyboard. The better your playing, the more likely you are to sense how even and how good everything feels.

Unresponsive
On some pianos, you press down a key and, for a split second, nothing seems to happen. If this is the case, you will also have little control over the tone, and the dynamic range will be limited. This can be a matter of poor regulation, and on used instruments it can be a sign of wear.

Regulate first
If you like the sound and the looks of an instrument, but not the feel, you can ask to have it regulated. Play it again after regulation, before you decide to buy the instrument.

Who needs a good action?
Some say that only good pianists need a truly good, quick, responsive action – but even as a novice you will play better if the instrument has a good, well-regulated action, so you'll probably play longer and enjoy it more. Again: If an instrument is only 'good enough to start on,' you may not get much further than starting.

Fast and responsive
On a grand piano, the hammer heads and the dampers simply fall back into place through gravity, when you let

go of the keys. That's one of the reasons why a grand piano action feels more responsive and gives you more control over the tone and the dynamics. It also explains why you can repeat notes more quickly on it, up to twelve times a second: A grand piano key doesn't have to come back up all the way before you can play it again. An upright key does, almost.

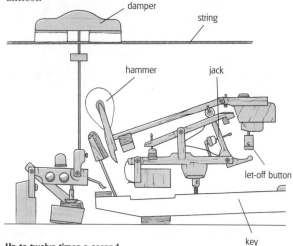

Up to twelve times a second...

Repetition mechanism

That's why, on most uprights, the repetition speed is limited to some eight or nine times a second – assuming you can even play that fast. That said, various manufacturers have devised systems to solve this problem. Such systems may work with a special repetition lever (Steingraeber), a set of magnets (SMR, a Dutch invention used by Seiler) or a spring (Sauter's R2 system or Fandrich's Vertical Action). These systems are standard on some makes and optional on others. They usually demand special regulation, and they can be more sensitive to changes in humidity (see page 93 and onwards). You won't usually find them in the lowest or highest price ranges.

Faster

With or without such systems, one piano may repeat faster than the next. How far the keys have to come back up before you can use them again may give you an indication of how fast an instrument can be played.

All the keys

If you have found an instrument that sounds and feels good, try all the keys one by one. Play them equally hard first, and then soft, and listen for rattles or buzzes. Also listen to what the dampers do: They must stop each note just as quickly and evenly. Please note that the highest fifteen to twenty notes don't have dampers (see next page).

Tricky legato

Dampers mustn't leave the string too late, nor must they return too quickly. If strings get muted again too soon, it is very hard to play legato, for instance, where each note has to flow into the next.

Wood or synthetic?

Synthetic action parts are quite widely used, especially but not exclusively in the lower price ranges. Modern varieties are very well suited to the job, being less sensitive to wear and changes in temperature and air humidity – but some pianists think they're less 'romantic' than their wooden counterparts.

Some of the synthetic parts used in the 1960s tended to become brittle. That's something to check, or have checked, if you buy a piano made in that period.

Brands

Actions are often built by specialized manufacturers, usually according to the specifications of the piano manufacturer. The best-known maker of actions is Renner. Other names include Defil, Langer, Pratt-Win, and Tofa.

HAMMERS AND DAMPERS

For a piano to sound, good it needs good hammer heads and precisely-regulated hammers. The same goes for the dampers.

Large heads

To set the long, thick bass strings in motion, you need big, heavy hammer heads, and equally big dampers to mute them again. As you go up the keyboard, hammer heads and dampers become gradually smaller.

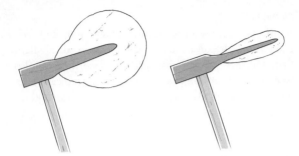

A hammer head for a bass string and one for the high notes.

No dampers
Tipcode PIANO-010

The strings of the highest one-and-a-half octaves vibrate so briefly that they don't need a damper at all. On most pianos, the last damper is somewhere between E6 and A6 (see page 13). The first key without a damper is often easy to find: simply play short notes in that area, key by key going upwards, until you hear the first note that goes on sounding when you let go of the key.

As small as possible

That transition must not be too big, but you do always hear the difference between the last note with, and the first note without, a damper. To make it as small as possible, most instruments are regulated so that the last damper only mutes very slightly.

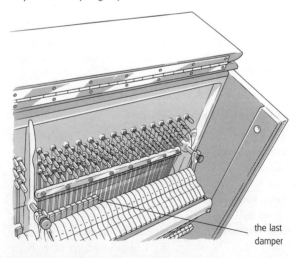

the last damper

The highest-sounding strings don't need dampers.

Just as high, just as far

On a well-regulated upright, the hammers are all at the same position along the strings: If a hammer strikes a string at a higher or lower point than it should, that note will sound noticeably different from the rest – especially with the high notes. All hammers must also be equally far from the strings: Uneven *hammer strokes* result in uneven dynamics.

Jam

Each space between hammers must always be equally wide. If hammers are too close together or do not move in a straight line, there's a chance that they will touch or even jam when you're playing. Also, a crooked hammer won't hit the string properly.

Extra string

Especially on very small uprights, a hammer may graze a string from the next note along. To check for this, use the sustaining pedal, play note for note, very slowly, and listen.

Voicing

For a good tone, the felt hammer heads should have the right hardness. If they're too hard, the tone will be brittle or edgy. Hammers that are too soft will make for a dull sound, lacking brightness. The process of making hammers harder or softer is called voicing.

Only so far

As it's not just the hammer heads which determine the tone, you can't expect voicing to completely alter the sound of an instrument. Want to know more? Turn to the secondhand buying tips on page 66 and the sections on tuning and regulation (pages 99 and 104).

Edgy

Voicing takes time. If it hasn't been done properly, a piano may start to sound noticeably harsher or edgier even after just a few months. Ultimately, every piano needs to be re-voiced.

Heavy felt

Some brochures mention exactly how heavy the felt of the

hammer heads is. On their own, such figures once again tell you little: The 'best' felt weight depends very much on the design of the whole instrument.

Brands

Abel and Renner are two well-known manufacturers of hammer heads.

STRINGS

Both uprights and grand pianos have around two hundred and twenty strings. Of course, all strings must be evenly

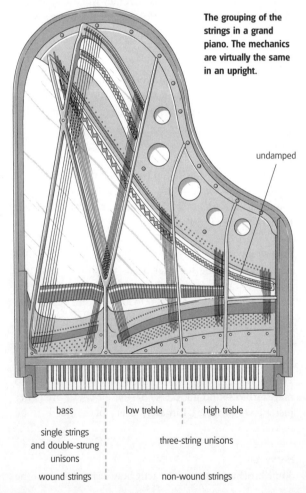

The grouping of the strings in a grand piano. The mechanics are virtually the same in an upright.

undamped

bass	low treble	high treble
single strings and double-strung unisons	three-string unisons	
wound strings	non-wound strings	

spaced across the instrument – but there is more to see and to know than that.

Twenty-five feet

Of the thinnest, highest strings, usually only a section of two or three inches (5–8 cm) actually vibrates. If the longest bass string were equally thin, it could only sound as low as it should if it were a good twenty or twenty-five feet long (7–8 meters).

Wound

This explains why these strings are a good deal thicker: The extra mass allows them to sound low enough without becoming too long. Lower sounding strings use heavier-gauge string wire, and the lowest strings are also wound with copper wire, in two or even three layers.

Single, double, and triple strings

The very lowest notes have only one string each. The higher-sounding bass notes are double-strung unisons: Each hammer strikes two strings at once. In the treble area there are three non-wound (*plain*) steel strings for each note.

Transition

Going from the bass strings to the low treble, three things change: The lower treble strings run across a different bridge, they are not wound, and there are three of them for each note. To make this transition as smooth as possible, the low treble section often starts with a few double-wound string unisons.

Listen

If the transition is really smooth, no note sounds noticeably fuller, warmer, or less bright than the one next to it. A tip for listening: Play the area where the number of strings per key change, note for note, very softly, and don't look at the strings. If you do, you may easily end up hearing what you see…

Scale

The word *scale* may refer to only the *speaking length* of the strings (the part that actually vibrates), but often it is also used to mean the precise number, the gauge, and the winding of the strings, and everything directly connected to it. In a piano featuring a *German scale design* the stringing is based on a German model – which tells you nothing about the quality of the instrument. On page 52 you can see roughly how the strings are grouped.

Smaller piano, thicker strings

The smaller a piano is, the thicker the strings need to be in order to produce the required pitches. That's one of the reasons why small pianos often sound less rich or full than tall instruments of the same quality: The thicker a string is, the stiffer it gets, and a stiff, short string doesn't vibrate as easily and freely as a thinner, longer string.

Shrill

On very small uprights pianos with poorer-quality strings, some notes can sound very shrill and slightly out of tune, even if the instrument is properly tuned. What you are then hearing is the *inharmonicity* of strings that are too stiff.

Replacing strings

Do you want to get the best from your instrument? After about twenty or thirty years, strings will have lost some of their tone and brightness, so you could have them replaced – but on most pianos, strings are replaced only after fifty years or more. Grand pianos in concert halls have their strings replaced much more often.

Loop strung

The three-string unisons are usually *loop strung*: One end of each length of string is fixed to a tuning pin, looped around the hitch pin and

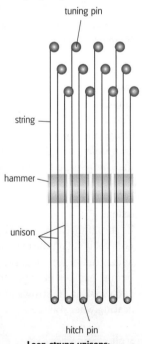

tuning pin

string

hammer

unison

hitch pin

Loop-strung unisons: One string length serves as two strings.

then fixed to the next tuning pin. In other words, that one string length serves as two strings.

Single stringing

There are only a few (expensive) brands that have three separate strings for a three-string unison. This is fairly easy to check on an open grand piano. If it has *single stringing*, each string is tied to the hitch pin.

Round, hexagonal, or octagonal

The string wires are just about always made in specialized factories. Well-known makes include Giese, Mapes, Poehlman, and Röslau. Winding the bass strings, on the other hand, is a job piano manufacturers often do themselves. The string wire of the wound is sometimes six- or eight-sided (hexagonal or octagonal, respectively), a feature that you can clearly see and feel along the non-wound parts of those strings. Such cores are said to make the winding easier and longer-lasting. Others say that a round core gives a more solid tone. The truth? You find both types in both the most expensive and in cheaper instruments, and again, in the end it's how the whole instrument sounds that counts.

From thick to thin

To give you an idea: the thickest strings are easily six or seven times as thick as the thinnest, and the speaking length can be twenty or thirty (!) times as long.

Tension

String tension is another parameter. Some makes apply higher string tensions than others. The construction of the instrument and the choice of strings play a role too. As an example, a relatively low string tension is said to give a more singing, sustained tone, while a high-tension scale would make for a brighter sound. Some experts also state that strings sound their best if they're as tight as can be, without breaking – and others disagree.

PINS, BLOCKS, AND BRIDGES

The strings run from the tuning pins to the hitch pins. On the way they pass not only the bridge, which transmits the vibrations to the soundboard, but also the pressure bar or a number of agraffes.

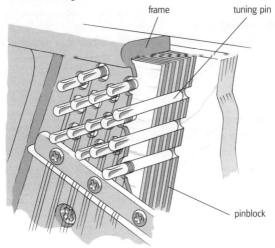

frame   tuning pin

pinblock

The pinblock is hidden behind the frame.

Pinblock
The pinblock, because it holds the tuning pins, has to take a whole lot of tension. That's why it's made up of laminated hardwood, the number of plies varying from three to thirty or more. This number doesn't say a thing about the quality of the block or the instrument: You'll find pinblocks with any number of plies in all price ranges.

Makes
Well-known pinblock manufacturers are Delignit and Dehonit, both from Germany. There are also piano manufacturers who make their own pinblocks. The quality of the pinblock is one the main things to influence the tuning stability of the instrument.

Slightly upwards
In order to withstand the tension of the strings, the tuning pins usually point slightly upward in an upright piano, and slightly towards the player in a grand. There must be some space between the string and the frame; only then can the string be tightened further if necessary. If a tuning pin comes slightly loose over the course of many years, the space allows it to be hammered a bit deeper into the pinblock.

A good pinblock

If you see that the tuning pins are not all set at the same angle, or if some pins are obviously deeper than others, there may be something wrong with the pinblock. Also, on a well-made piano, the tuning pins are set far enough apart that the strings don't touch each other at any point.

Bridges

A violin has a small, thin wooden bridge, which transmits the vibrations of the strings to the body, where they are amplified. Pianos work in just the same way, on that point at least: Two bridges pass on the vibrations to the soundboard, which amplifies the sound. There's a separate

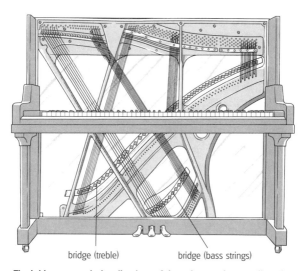

bridge (treble)   bridge (bass strings)

The bridges transmit the vibrations of the strings to the soundboard...

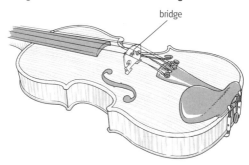

bridge

... just as a violin bridge transmits the vibrations of the strings to the body.

short bridge for the bass strings; the other strings use the *treble bridge* or *long bridge*.

Bridge pins
The better the contact between bridge and strings, the better the result will be. That's why the strings run zigzag across the bridge, kept in place by the *bridge pins*. These small metal pins also help to transmit the vibrations.

Pressure bar
From the tuning pins, the strings either run under a metal *pressure bar*, or through small brass studs, known as *agraffes*. The agraffes, having one hole per string length, assure that the strings are spaced at the right distance from each other – which is mainly convenient for the person who fits the strings.

Agraffes
Almost all grand pianos have agraffes for the bass strings and the low treble, and a pressure bar for the high treble. This bar is also known as *capo d'astro* or *capo bar*. On upright pianos you find almost all combinations in almost all price ranges – agraffes throughout, a pressure bar for all the strings, or perhaps agraffes only for the bass strings. In other words, the use of agraffes or pressure bars says nothing about the quality or price of the instrument.

The ends
The ends of the strings – the parts near the tuning pins at

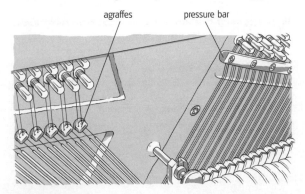

Agraffes for the bass strings, and a pressure bar for the higher-sounding strings.

one end and the hitch pins at the other – do not belong to the *speaking length* of the string. Even so, they do vibrate along, very softly. That can be disturbing, especially on the lower strings, which is why a strip of felt is usually threaded between the ends of those strings.

Duplex scale

In many grand pianos, however, the end parts of the higher-sounding strings are used to enhance the tone: With the help of small metal 'ridges', these sections are set so that they are in tune with the speaking lengths of the strings – a Steinway invention which is called *duplex scale*.

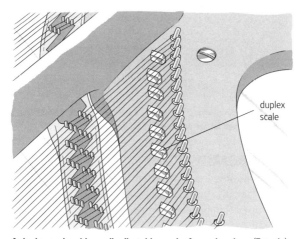

A duplex scale with small adjustable combs for each unison (Estonia).

Less bright

You can easily hear how important those vibrations at the ends of the strings are. First play a note, then put a finger to muffle the end part of the appropriate string, and play the note again. It'll sound less bright the second time.

Aliquot scale

The German company Blüthner has another method to make the highest octaves sound a little richer: All the three-string unisons have a fourth string added. This string is not struck by the hammer, but if you play quite loudly, it does vibrate along sympathetically. The name of this *aliquot scale* comes from the French *son aliquot*, which means *harmonic* or *overtone*.

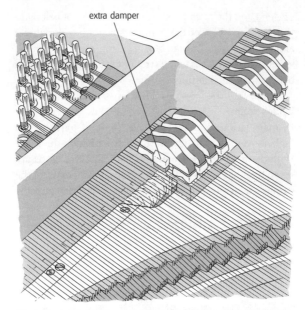

extra damper

Aliquot scale: four strings per unison. Each damper has a small extra damper attached for the fourth string (Blüthner).

SOUNDBOARD

The soundboard is often referred to as the soul or the voice of the instrument. Usually, this large wooden plate is made up of thin planks of spruce. It is no coincidence that this is the same type of wood used for the tops of violins and many guitars.

Grain

For a good tone, the vibrations need to be able to pass through the whole soundboard very quickly. Vibrations move fastest if the wood has a fine, straight grain. This wood is found especially in Alaska, Siberia, and other cold regions, where trees grow very slowly, developing the desired grain.

Crown

The soundboard isn't perfectly flat. On a grand, its center rises up about a third of an inch; on an upright it curves slightly toward the keyboard. This curve, called the *crown* or *belly*, keeps the wood under tension, which contributes to the tone.

Ribs

The ribs on the soundboard are perpendicular to the grain of the wood, which helps to distribute the vibrations across the soundboard faster. The ribs also help maintain the soundboard's shape.

A bit flatter

After many years, most soundboards do get a bit flatter, and that can make the tone a bit flatter too. On the other hand: however important the crown is, there are plenty of instruments, old and new, which sound excellent but have no crown at all, or one which is barely noticeable.

Cracks

The forces on the soundboard can not only flatten it in time, but it may crack too. This can even occur very rapidly if the wood shrinks or expands a lot – for instance, if it is exposed to rapid changes in temperature or humidity. Eventually, after half a century or more, just about every soundboard will develop cracks. Fortunately, in most cases the piano's performance will not suffer from them. There's more about cracked soundboards – and how to prevent them – on page 69, and on page 92 and onwards.

From thick to thin

Most soundboards are about a third of an inch (1 cm) thick at the high treble, where they preferably show a very fine grain. That makes the wood a bit stiffer, which in turn helps the highest frequencies to sound good. At the side of the bass strings, the soundboard is often a little thinner with a coarser grain, which enhances the lower frequencies. All kinds of ideas have been developed to help soundboards to 'sing.' For instance, there are soundboards with a groove around them, which supposedly allows them to vibrate more freely.

Bigger? Maybe not...

Larger instruments can sound 'bigger' because they have a bigger soundboard, among other reasons. You can't always tell from the outside, however. Some manufacturers make vertical pianos with a tall cabinet that houses a relatively small soundboard, for instance. Conversely, some companies make their grands a bit wider, which allows for a slightly larger soundboard than in other grands of comparable size.

Laminated soundboards

Instead of a soundboard made of solid planks of wood, many instruments have a laminated one. The earliest laminated soundboards were mostly used in pianos that were very cheap and not especially good. These days, there are also instruments available with laminated soundboards that are built well and sound good. Still, you won't find this type of soundboard in the very best instruments: A good solid soundboard contributes to a richer tone. On the other hand, laminated soundboards are very resistant to changes in humidity and temperature, and they don't crack or go flat.

How to tell

You can often tell a laminated soundboard by looking at the grain at the back and inside the instrument. If it runs in different directions, it's laminated wood. Also, if the grain runs straight down instead of diagonally, you are looking at a laminated soundboard.

PEDALS

Most uprights and grand pianos have three pedals. Only the one on the right has the same function on both instruments.

Damper pedal   Tipcode PIANO-011

This pedal is called the sustain(ing) pedal because it allows the strings to sustain by lifting all the dampers simultaneously – which explains its second name, *damper pedal*.

Different sound

When you use this pedal, the timbre of the instruments changes too, as the strings of the keys you don't play vibrate along softly with everything you do play. Play the

Middle C (C4)   C5 E5 G5

Play long notes: first without, then with the sustain pedal.

chord shown here and keep the keys pressed down a little while. Let them go. Now press down the sustain pedal, then play the same thing. You'll hear the difference.

At the same time
When you press the pedal down, check whether all the dampers leave the strings at the same time. If you use this pedal a lot, you're likely to keep your foot resting on it lightly. For this reason, the dampers mustn't respond immediately, but only when you press the pedal down a little further. A good pedal allows you to control the dampers very precisely, moving them to and from the strings as fast or as slowly as the music requires.

Rattles and buzzes
Also listen for any unwanted extra noises, with each pedal. For example, play a chord loudly with the sustain pedal pressed down, and then let the pedal come back up very slowly. Are all the notes damped equally and at the same time? Are there any rattles, buzzes, or squeaks?

Half-blow pedal
The soft pedal of an upright piano is also known as *half-blow pedal*: It moves the hammers closer to the strings, and the reduced hammer stroke results in a softer tone.

A different feel
Using the soft pedal also makes the piano feel slightly different: When the hammers are moved forwards, a tiny bit of space opens up above the jack (see the illustration on page 45). As a result, the jack has to bridge this space before setting the hammer in motion. This makes the keyboard feel uneven and less responsive, and it reduces your control over the tone. The effect is worse on some instruments than on others.

The middle pedal   Tipcode PIANO-003
The middle pedal of an upright is often a muffler pedal, also known as practice pedal, *mute pedal, celeste pedal,* and *moderator stop.* It lowers a strip of felt between the hammers and the strings, which substantially reduces the volume. Unfortunately, it also makes the instrument feel quite different, as the felt changes the rebound of the hammers.

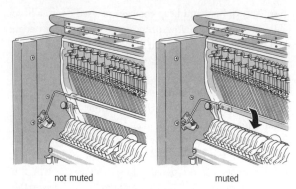

not muted   muted

A strip of felt between hammers and strings...

Locked

Most practice pedals can be locked in the 'on' position, either by moving the pedal a little to the left when pressing it down, or by simply pressing it down once, later releasing it by pressing it once more.

By hand

There are hand-operated versions as well. Most of these models have a lever, usually hidden under the keyboard. The most basic versions require you to open the lid to lower or raise the felt. These types of mufflers can rather easily be retrofit into most upright pianos. Practice mutes on grands are very rare.

Mute rail   Tipcode PIANO-012

The middle pedal can have other functions too. If the piano has a sound module, the pedal may be used to lower a rubber clad bar or rail (usually known as *mute rail* or *hammer-stop rail*) which stops the hammers from hitting the strings. This allows you to practice in complete silence (Hybrid pianos; see Chapter 7).

Many instruments have either a mute rail or a muffler, and some have both, one being operated with a lever, the other with a pedal.

Bass sustain

On some instruments the middle pedal lifts the dampers in the bass register only. Such a *bass sustain pedal* is only really useful if all the notes you want to sustain happen to be in the bass – which is rarely so.

Ornamental

… and on some cheaper uprights the third pedal is purely ornamental – either it does nothing at all, or it does the same as the soft pedal.

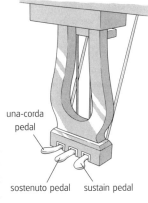

una-corda pedal

sostenuto pedal   sustain pedal

A lyre-shaped lyre.

Grands and lyres

The lyre is the part of a grand piano that holds the pedals. On some grands, it actually has the shape of a lyre.

Not just softer...   Tipcode PIANO-006

When using the una-corda pedal of a grand piano, the sound gets a bit softer because one less string is struck in each unison. But that isn't all.

... but milder too

Where the strings normally come into contact with the hammers, they make grooves in the felt, so that the felt becomes a little denser and harder there. If you use the una-corda pedal, the strings are struck by the softer part of the hammer, just beside those grooves. This also changes the tone, making it sound a little milder, softer, or more nasal, as some say.

One out of two strings

The term 'una corda' (meaning 'one string') stems from the early days of the instrument. Back then, there were two strings for each note: Of those two, only one was struck if you used the una-corda system.

One less, one more

When you press the una-corda pedal, the hammers should move far enough to the side so that they really do strike one fewer string in each unison, without grazing one of the strings in the next unison. If you press down the keys very slowly one by one, you can clearly see whether the hammers are striking where they should, and if you listen closely, you can hear it too.

Sostenuto pedal
Tipcode PIANO-007

Nearly all modern grand pianos have a sostenuto pedal (see page 12); many older models don't. Does that matter? There isn't much music which requires this third pedal. In certain works by Bach you can use it to sustain some of the low notes, which is why it's sometimes called a *Bach pedal*. Another name is a *Steinway pedal*, because this company acquired the patent to the original sostenuto pedal invented by Pleyel in 1875.

And very occasionally...

Some uprights can be ordered with a sostenuto pedal for an additional charge. On old instruments you may come across a *bass sostenuto*, which obviously works only in the lowest register.

Four pedals

The Italian brand Fazioli makes grands with a fourth pedal, which works in just about the same way as the soft pedal of an upright piano, yet without its disadvantages (see page 63).

SECONDHAND

It's hard to judge a secondhand piano properly – certainly not if it's an older instrument in somebody's home. Even so, there are all kinds of things you can check for yourself, in addition to what was discussed above, before reaching the point that you need to consult with an expert to appraise an instrument you really like (see page 23).

Play, look and listen

When you are playing, listen out especially for rattles or buzzes, watch out for keys that are hard work to play, or that creak or squeak, and for hammers which double-strike when you play softly. Feel to check that there are no keys that can move sideways too easily. The greatest wear is usually in the middle part of the keyboard: That's where pianos get played the most.

Very light

If a piano plays very, very easily, this may indicate excessive wear, lack of regulation, or both: The action of a badly regulated piano will wear faster. If either one is the case, it will usually be hard or impossible to play really softly, the volume will be difficult to control, and the action is noisy.

Inside
Have a look inside too. Ask the person selling the piano to remove lamps, vases, and other items from the instrument, and to open the lid, thus preventing breaking or damaging things yourself.

Hammers
Check whether all the hammers of an upright are lined up and at equal distances from the strings (see page 51). Hold down different groups of keys and look to see whether the hammers stay in line. When you let the keys go, the hammers should all fall back at the same time.

Heads with grooves
Grooves in the hammer heads are normal on a used piano. Look especially carefully at the hammer heads in the middle section: They usually have the most to put up with. The grooves should never be near the edge of the head, but roughly in the middle. The strings should fall exactly into those grooves: You can check that by pressing the keys down very softly.

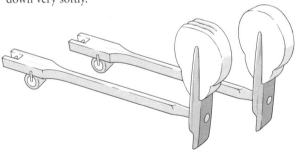

A worn-out hammer head with deep grooves, and a new head.

Deep grooves and moths
If the grooves are very deep, the hammer heads can be sanded back into shape – if the felt is still thick enough, and if it hasn't dried out too much. Take another look at the hammers: Moths have a taste for felt. Replacing hammer heads easily costs six hundred dollars or more.

Strings

Rusty strings? If so, the piano may have been kept in a very damp room. That can be a problem if you move it to a house with low air humidity (see page 93). Rust also causes a dull tone, and rusty strings are harder to tune. If you find new strings between a whole bunch of old ones, it can be a sign that more strings are going to break.

Properly tuned

Like a new piano, you can only judge a secondhand piano if it's properly tuned. If a piano is flat (too low) over the whole range, it won't sound out of tune – but it will be a problem if you want to play with others. Besides, a piano sounds best when tuned to the right pitch. Last but not least, a piano that sounds a half-tone (half-step) or more too low usually can't be tuned back up to the right pitch with one tuning. So how can you check the general pitch?

A=440

Pianos should be tuned so that the strings of A4 (see page 13) vibrate 440 times per second. This is known as A=440 hertz or A=440.

Tuning fork   Tipcode PIANO-013

An affordable way to check this is to use a tuning fork – a small metal fork that sounds a very clear pitch. Tuning forks, available for a few dollars, come in various pitches. Get one which is labeled A=440. Tap the tuning fork against your knee and hold the stem against the cabinet or against your ear. Play A4 and compare the two pitches. If the piano's tone sounds much lower, it may need special care to get it back to the proper pitch (see page 101).

A tuning fork.

Tuner

You can use an electronic tuner instead. The built-in microphone 'hears' the pitch, and a series of LEDs or a pointer tells you whether the tone is in tune, flat, or sharp. Most guitarists and bassists have one, if you don't.

An expert eye

Judging the condition of important wooden parts (soundboard, pinblock, bridges) and the action requires an expert eye – unless the damage is so bad that you can see it too. Check that the tuning pins are all at the same angle, that the ribs are touching the soundboard all along their length, and that they are not cracked. Should the soundboard need to be replaced (one or even more cracks, even clearly visible ones, do not make that a necessity *per se*), it's worth knowing that such an operation easily costs as much as a decent new piano... Crooked panels? Then there's a good chance that the soundboard is no longer in shape.

Woodworm

Small holes in the wood? Could be woodworm. Woodworms don't like music, so if a piano is played often, it's probably not inhabited.

Overdamper

If you come across a vertical piano that has dampers above the hammers, you can assume it's probably over a hundred years old. Don't spend too much money on this type of piano, which is known as an *overdamper*.

Straight-strung

Another type to be wary of is the *straight-strung upright*, on which the strings run vertically. They are usually very old and not worth much. Exceptions are some uprights by the Dutch make Rippen; this factory was still building straight-strung instruments up until the 1980s.

Age

If you want to know exactly how old an instrument is, you can find tables with serial numbers and year of construction for nearly all makes in the *Pierce Piano Atlas* and similar books. Many piano stores have a copy you can consult. You can find lists like this on the Internet too (see page 132). The serial number is often shown on the frame, but it may be under the lid, on the pinblock, or on the soundboard as well. A tip: Some components have their own serial or other numbers too, so make sure you pick the right one.

6. PLAY-TESTING

This chapter supplements Chapter 5, concentrating on choosing an instrument by ear. Tips for playing, even if you can't really play yet, tips to hear the difference between one instrument and the next, and tips that help you listen more consciously.

In a store, everything sounds different than it does at home. If you ask the salesperson to first let you hear a very bright sounding piano, followed by one with a mellow, warm sound, you'll get an idea of how different instruments can sound in the acoustics of the store. The prices of those instruments are not the point right now.

Start with the extremes

These two extremes are also a good starting point if you don't yet have a clear idea of the sound you're looking for. Decide which of the two appeals to you most, and carry on from there. Another tip: You can also play (or get someone to play) the cheapest and the most expensive piano in the store right after each other, or try one model in each price range. That may give you a better picture of the price-related differences between instruments, and of what you can and should listen out for.

Your own piano

Another starting point is the instrument you already have – if you already have one. Some piano salespeople will come to your home, to see the room where the instrument will be played in, and to check out the instrument you are currently playing, and its value.

Loud or soft

An instrument sounds much louder and brighter in a room with hard acoustics (wooden floor, little furniture) than in a room with thick rugs and curtains. You need to take that into account when making a choice. The tone can be adjusted slightly (voicing; pages 51, and 104–105), but don't expect anyone to turn a piano with a decidedly bright tone into a very warm, romantic-sounding instrument.

Impressive

Many piano stores have quite hard acoustics, in which instruments tend to sound quite impressive even if you are a half-decent pianist, and especially if you use the sustain pedal a lot and open the lid wide.

Someone else

Most piano salespeople know how to play the instrument. Even so, if you haven't been playing very long yourself, it can be a good idea to take another pianist along on one of your visits – preferably one who can play what you would like to play yourself, and most importantly someone who will show you what the *piano* can do, rather than what *they* can do.

Quite wrong

Even if you do play, having a second pianist along can't do any harm. Then you can get the other person to play, so that you can concentrate on listening better. Or you can let that other person play without you seeing which instrument they are playing – and you may find you are quite wrong about which piano you think you are listening to…

Comparing

Choosing instruments on their tone and timbre is primarily a question of comparing. The first piano you play may sound great straightaway – but often you'll only really be able to judge if you play a couple of other instruments right afterwards.

At home

If you are buying at somebody's home, there's nothing to compare the piano with. This makes it even more important to take another player along.

PLAYING

If you sit down to play in a store, try not to wonder what the staff thinks of your playing. They shouldn't be listening to *how* you play but to *what* you play, in order to be of as much help as possible in choosing an instrument that suits you.

Briefly

If you have a lot of pianos to choose from, it may be best to start by playing only briefly on each instrument. Once you have narrowed down your choice to a manageable number, compare them two by two or three by three. Discard the one you like least and choose another in its place. And so on. Naturally, you'll want to play longer when you're down to fewer instruments.

Simple

To start with, play simple things – otherwise you'll be concentrating more on playing than on listening. Even just scales and chords can give a good first impression.

D-minor chord (D-minor 7)

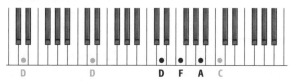

D   D   D F A C

G-major chord (G7)

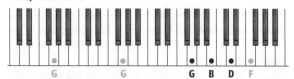

G   G   G B D F

C-major chord (C-major 7)

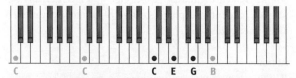

C   C   C E G B

Three great-sounding test chords. Either play the keys with the black dots only, or include the other keys as well.

Even if you can't play
Tipcode PIANO-014

The chords shown on the previous page will give you a fair impression of how a piano sounds. Even if you don't really play, you can play them – after all, playing a chord is no more than playing a few keys at the same time. To begin with, choose one of the three chords and play only the keys with the black dots. If you're more than a novice, then play the keys with the gray dots too. These three chords will sound best if you play them in the order shown, one after the other.

Long notes

Very short notes often tell you less about the tone of an instrument than long notes. Play both.

High, middle, and low
Tipcode PIANO-015

Another simple playing and listening tip: Play the same three-note chord at different places on the keyboard. Start off high and go down from there, or the other way around, or both. Also, play it loud and soft, sustain the notes or play them very shortly (staccato).

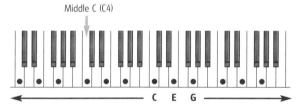

Middle C (C4)

C E G

One chord, played along the entire keyboard (C-major).

Same chord, different instrument

A variation: Take that same chord and play it on the same keys, but on different pianos. If you try putting what you hear into words, the differences may be easier to remember. Think of words like velvety or bright, warm, full, mellow, transparent, solid, nasal, rich, thin, or shrill – or think in colors: One piano may sound 'browner' to you, another one may have a shade of blue…

Color

Pianists often talk about color in a different way too: The better the instrument is, the more (tonal) colors or timbres it allows you to play – provided you play well enough.

Play longer

You'll naturally want to play longer on those instruments from which you are going to make your final choice. Listening is easiest if you play pieces you know well. Try to play a wide variety of things, from loud to soft, with and without pedals, and from as fast as you can to notes that last a minute each.

Empty music desk

If you are used to playing from sheet music, take some pieces with you when you go to choose a piano.

LISTENING

You can't learn how to listen just by reading about it, but you can read about what to listen out for.

Even progression

Of course the high notes on a piano sound different than the low notes, but the progression should be very even. Nor should the transitions be too large, for instance from the bass notes to the low treble (page 53), or from the high notes with dampers to the ones without (page 50).

Soft and loud

On a good piano you can play very softly and still get what you want from every note. You can also play very loudly without the sound distorting or becoming metallic or thinnish, or the notes blurring together so that no one can really hear what you're playing anymore. An instrument that can do all this has good dynamics.

Louder and brighter

As you start playing harder, the instrument not only starts sounding louder, but brighter too. The degree and evenness of that change differ per instrument.

Try a grand too

Grand pianos generally have a bigger dynamic range than uprights – you can make a grand sound both softer and louder. Choosing an upright? Try listening to what a good grand piano can do too, just so you know what's the maximum you can expect from an instrument.

**A bigger dynamic
range than an upright...**

The lower notes

The differences in character between different instruments
often is most obvious in the lowest octaves. Keep playing
the same chord in the same lower octave, equally loudly or
softly, on different instruments.

Every note

In the very lowest range, check that every separate note
stands out, even if you play fast phrases. Also, in a good
instrument you can almost feel the bass notes, and a good
low note doesn't drone. It sounds.

High

The highest notes always sound short, but they should still
sing. 'Plink' is not enough. Good pianos have bright, full-
sounding highs. Lesser instruments may sound edgy, shrill,
or thin in the high treble area.

Middle

The low treble is the area where you'll play the most – and
it's also the area where pianos tend to sound very much
alike. But when you're really playing, you'll certainly hear
the difference between one instrument and the next –
even within that range.

Singing

The difference between a piano that can 'sing' and one that can't is quite easy to hear. A listening tip: If you play a chord or two notes at once on a good instrument and keep the keys pressed down, you'll often notice that the sound seems to start singing just after you play the keys – as though the notes are reinforcing each other. You can hear this effect most clearly in the bass.

The attack

It's also important to listen to what happens at the very moment the hammers strike the strings. Much of the difference in tone between one instrument and the next lies in that sound, the *attack*. The attack can be very bright, or be soft, warm, mushy, firm, indistinct, aggressive, or massive – to give just a few examples.

Bright or warm

Pianists often divide pianos into two broad groups: the bright-sounding instruments on the one hand and the warm-sounding ones on the other. Asian-built pianos are usually placed in the first category, European instruments in the second, American pianos somewhere in between. However, there may be as many exceptions to this rule as there are pianos – or pianists…

Taste

When two people listen to the same piano, they'll often use very different words to describe what they hear. What one finds shrill (and so not attractive), another may describe as bright (and so not unattractive), and what's warm and romantic to one ear sounds dull or lifeless to another. It all depends on what you like – and the words you use to describe it.

Style

What you like often coincides with what you play. Jazz musicians often choose a brighter-sounding instrument, for example. A thundering, heavily orchestrated piece may sound better on one piano, and something airy and fast better on another; and a large choir may require a different piano sound than a salsa band. In other words, there's no such thing as the best piano.

7. HYBRID, PLAYER, AND DIGITAL PIANOS

Digital technique allows you to play a regular piano in complete silence, to hook pianos up to a computer, or to have pianos play by themselves. An introduction to the possibilities, from sound modules and effects to MIDI.

Tipcode PIANO-012

Pianos can be provided with a system that allows you to play using a sound module and headphones, the hammers being stopped from hitting the strings by a pedal or lever-operated rail. Pianos with this feature are known as *hybrid pianos*: They're both acoustic and digital instruments. Expect to pay an additional two thousand dollars or more for a hybrid piano, the exact price depending, for one thing, on the features of the sound module.

Names

Many piano brands have their own 'silent' system. Their trade names often describe their purpose: Anytime, City Piano, DuoVox, Night & Day, MIDIPiano (formerly known as Silent Piano), StillAcoustic, QuietTime, and VARIO System are some examples.

Just like an acoustic

The sound modules that come with such systems faithfully reproduce the 'real' instrument. The volume goes up if you play harder, and the other way around; the pedals will affect the sound and the feel the same way, and so on. The main differences are that the sound doesn't come from the strings and the soundboard; the sounds are samples (digital recordings of the 'real' instrument), which are amplified and then conveyed through a pair of headphones.

Optical sensors

To trigger the sounds, the movements of the keys are picked up by sensors. Usually these are optical sensors, one under each key, which respond to minute light beams, as this type of sensor doesn't affect the feel of the piano. However, the keyboard will feel slightly different when the mute rail has been activated; the hammers travel less far than when they *do* hit the strings.

A sound module with extensive options (Technics).

Simple

The most basic sound modules have only a volume control and one or two headphone outputs. Having two headphone outputs is handy for lessons or playing duets.

More sounds   Tipcode PIANO-016

More elaborate models usually offer more sounds. Besides samples of one or more grand pianos or uprights, they may feature electric pianos, a few organs, a harpsichord, a choir, or a set of violins (strings). Other modules offer you the choice between hundreds of different instruments.

Piano sounds

In the end, most pianists use mainly the piano sounds, or just one of them. So pay special attention to the quality of those sounds, just as you would listen to acoustic pianos. There can be considerable differences between different makes.

Metronome and reverb   Tipcode PIANO-017

If a metronome is featured on the module, it is helpful if it has a volume control. Some modules have built-in effects. A *reverb* is quite common, adding a little life and space to the digital piano sound. If the module has more sounds, there usually are types of effects too – a *chorus*, for instance, which is often used to make an electric piano sound slightly fuller.

Recording

A built-in digital *sequencer* or *recorder* records what you play. So, for example, you can record the right-hand part of a piece, play it back, and then play the left-hand part along to it. Or you can play back what you have just recorded simply to hear what you sounded like. Or you can record an idea for your own piece, or play a duet on your own…

Many sound modules have special outputs (*line out* or *audio out*) to connect the module to a stereo system – so you can listen without headphones too.

Audio in

An input for sound signals (marked *line in* or *audio in*) can be used to hook up a CD player or another audio source to the piano, so you play along with other recordings without disturbing anyone.

Operation

Some sound modules have all the controls on the box itself; others have the most important controls to the left of the keyboard or elsewhere closer at hand. These may be easier to reach, but they're also more visible.

Polyphony

Often, brochures will say something about the number of notes that the sound module can produce at the same time. If the module offers *16-voice polyphony*, it can play sixteen notes at once. That sounds like a lot – you only have ten fingers – but in fact you'll often need more. After all, if you sustain a chord and carry on playing other notes, you soon use more than ten sounds or voices simultaneously. Basically, 64-voice polyphony should always give you enough capacity, whatever you play.

Expanded possibilities

Most sound modules allow you to expand the possibilities of your piano in another way too: You can now hook it up to a computer, a synthesizer, or any other electronic instrument.

Computer

If you connect your piano to a computer, you can have the computer print out what you play in notes, you can record your performance (including strings, brass, percussion, and any other instrument) and edit it later, or you can use the computer as a teacher – all provided your computer has the software and the hardware to do so.

Piano keys, synthesizer sounds

If you link a synthesizer to your sound module, you can produce the sounds of that synthesizer by playing the keys of your piano. You can turn it around too, playing the sounds from your module using the synth's keyboard.

MIDI

All this is made possible by a system called MIDI, which stands for *Musical Instrument Digital Interface*. Basically, MIDI translates the notes you play (and their loudness and other data) into standardized codes. These codes can be 'read' and converted to sound by any type of device that uses MIDI.

MIDI out

The simplest sound modules only have a MIDI output. This allows you to control other instruments from your piano, or to record your performance on your computer.

MIDI in

A MIDI input allows you to send MIDI data to your sound module – so you can control its sounds from another keyboard, for instance, or you can use your module to play back what you recorded on your computer.

MIDI thru

A third type of connector is MIDI thru, which allows you to include the instrument in a daisy-chain of MIDI equipment.

More information

There's much more about sound modules, sequencers, and MIDI in other Tipbooks (see page 138).

PLAYER PIANOS

Player pianos can play by themselves. Basically, they're not very different from hybrid pianos. What sets them apart is that player pianos have a jack under the very end of every key. These jacks (*solenoids*) are controlled by the sound module, which activates the keys, thus replacing the pianist's fingers, which would normally play the piano.

Record...

The idea is very simple. A pianist plays a piece on an instrument with built-in sensors that register all the key and pedal movements very precisely. The performance is recorded digitally.

... and reproduce

Afterwards, the process is reversed. The player system converts the digital recording to signals that 'tell' the jacks exactly which keys to play and how hard. The pedals are operated in much the same way. The result is a modern player piano: a piano that plays itself. These systems don't come cheap; they can cost as much as five to eight thousand dollars.

Famous pianists

Player pianos can be used to record and reproduce your own playing, but you can also bring famous pianists into your living room, as a recording stored on floppy disk, CD, or other media – and on a real instrument they'll always sound better than on even the best hi-fi system. Or you can let a master pianist play the right-hand part, while you play the left-hand part yourself. Most new computer techniques and storage systems are quickly finding their way into these types of systems.

Brands

Four well-known player piano systems are ConcertMaster (Baldwin), Disklavier (Yamaha), PianoDisc, and QRS/Pianomation.

DIGITAL PIANOS

As an alternative or in addition to an acoustic piano, you can get a digital piano. Some digital pianos look very much like the real thing; others, so-called *stage pianos*, look more like a home keyboard or a synthesizer.

A good keyboard

To make good digital pianos feel like their acoustic counterparts, small hammers are often built into their actions, their only function being to provide the desired feel. These keyboards come with names such as *hammer action*, *hammered action*, and *weighted action*. Some digital grands even have a genuine grand piano action.

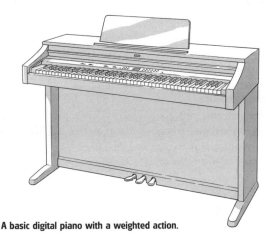

A basic digital piano with a weighted action.

Touch-sensitive

Of course, a digital piano has to be *touch-sensitive*: The sound gets louder if you play harder – and not only louder, but a little brighter too, just like an acoustic piano.

Not quite the same sound

However good a digital piano is, it will never sound the same as an acoustic piano. One of the main reasons is that the sound comes from a set of speakers, rather than being produced by a soundboard.

No strings

Digital pianos also sound different because they don't have strings, and non-existent strings can't 'sing' along, for instance when you press the sustain pedal. This makes the sound of the digital instrument noticeably less resonant. Today, however, this effect is being simulated in a growing number of models.

Learning to play

Even then, you still learn to play better on a good acoustic piano than on a digital one – and the difference between acoustic and digital instruments gets bigger the better your technique gets.

Options

Most digital pianos have more options than the sound modules usually installed in acoustic pianos: more sounds, more effects, a recorder that can do more (more tracks, a larger memory, editing facilities), and so on. MIDI and other inputs and outputs are now practically standard.

The price

Digital pianos cost less than acoustic ones. A good-sounding digital piano with a piano-like action will set you back some fifteen hundred dollars, and some cost even less. For some three to seven thousand dollars you can get yourself the very best, with numerous sounds and all the options you could wish for. On the other hand, digital instruments don't last as long as acoustic pianos, and they lose their value a lot sooner. Then again, digital instruments need no maintenance and don't have to be tuned, voiced, or regulated.

8. ACCESSORIES

An introduction to some of the main accessories for piano players: piano benches and stools, piano lamps, caster cups, and – if you need to sound a bit louder – pickups.

Most pianists prefer rectangular benches rather than the smaller, round seat of a stool. Benches – which may offer sheet music storage under the seat – and stools are both available in hard-top and upholstered or padded versions. Hard-top seats can be made more comfortable with separately available bench pads. The most luxurious benches, often featuring a diamond tuffed vinyl or even leather upholstery, are known as *artist benches*.

Upholstery
If you decide to go for a padded version, then note that a leather upholstery is very luxurious, but vinyl is easier to keep clean, and fabric is less sticky and sweaty than vinyl. A selection of colors is available, with black being the most popular.

Height-adjustable
Playing is easier and less tiring if you are sitting at the right height. Not all benches are height-adjustable; most stools are. Usually, the difference between the highest and the lowest position is some three to six inches. Some seats can be adjusted as low as 16" or as high as 25".

Non-adjustable
Non-adjustable benches are available in different heights,

to match either the player or the instrument: *Grand benches* may be about an inch lower than *upright benches*, as the keys of a grand piano are a bit lower than those of an upright. Grand benches are often a little wider too.

Knobs or a spring

Artist benches have two large knobs to adjust the height. Others systems use a spring, and if you have to adjust the height very often, when different people use the instrument, a bench with a pneumatic system may be the solution.

Spinning the seat

Stools are adjusted by spinning the seat. Usually this means that you'll have to re-adjust the height from time to time, as the seat also spins a little when you stand up or sit down – but there are stools that are designed to prevent that. Expect to pay around a hundred and fifty dollars or more for a good stool that won't wobble after years of use.

Chairs

Some players prefer a stool, which has the added comfort of a back rest. Piano chairs are available in adjustable and non-adjustable versions. Some stools have shorter front legs, so the seat slopes toward the piano.

Legs

To make a bench perfectly match your piano and your interior, some companies offer a choice of leg styles,

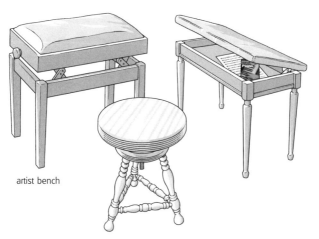

artist bench

ranging from Queen Anne and Louis XV to square-tapered or brass ferrule variations, and many more.

More expensive

A good bench will easily cost you two to three hundred dollars, but there are adjustable benches for as little as a hundred dollars. Extra money may buy you extra sturdiness, a longer lifespan, or just a more exclusive design. Some people take exclusivity to extremes: There are benches which sell for over two thousand dollars. Other specialties include *duet benches* on which you can adjust the height of both seats separately, or benches with a seat which you can tip forwards slightly.

LAMPS

Most piano lamps are fairly classical, brass designs, but others have a more modern look. Both types come with halogen lamps or ordinary bulbs. For grand pianos, there are special versions that you can clamp to the music desk. If the lamp needs to stand on the back part of an upright's lid, because the front part is open for playing, then a model with a boom arm can be handy. Piano lamps easily cost one to four hundred dollars. The difference between a piano lamp and an ordinary one is that the first usually has two light bulbs, which distribute the light across the entire keyboard.

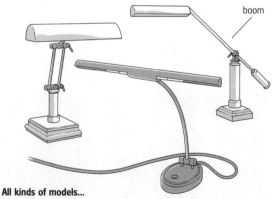

boom

All kinds of models...

CASTER CUPS

Casters, small ones especially, tend to leave deep marks in

most types of carpet. The solution: a set of caster cups. Of course, the cups should be removed when you want to use the casters to move the piano.

All kinds of materials
Caster cups are available in all kinds of materials (wood, plastic, glass) and finishes (satin or high-gloss; walnut, ebony, mahogany, etc.) to match the instrument or the floor. Prices range from about twenty to more than fifty dollars for a set of three cups.

Reduce the sound
Caster cups may help reducing the sound a piano transmits to the floor, and there are special caster cups which have been designed for that purpose.

Too low
If the keyboard of a piano is very low – or if you are very tall, or both – the whole instrument can be placed onto extra high caster cups. A tip: The higher the caster cups are, the harder it will be to comfortably reach the pedals.

... in various materials and heights...

PICKUPS
If you often have to play amplified – in a band, for instance – you can use one or two good quality (vocal) microphones, aimed at the soundboard. *Acoustic pickups* often work much better, though.

Vibration-sensitive
Pickups or *transducers* are thin strips or discs which literally 'pick up' the vibrations of the instrument and

convert them to electric signals, which are sent to the amplifier. Similar products are used on acoustic guitars, violins, and other instruments. On a piano it's best to stick one or two to the soundboard, between the ribs. Usually, one pickup won't be capable to truly capture the entire range of the instrument.

Where to put them

Where you need to put the pickups to get the best results may vary per instrument and per type of pickup. Most manuals supply tips on this subject. If not, ask your dealer.

Pricing

A set of two good piano pickups will easily cost some three to five hundred dollars or more, including a small preamp which boosts the signal before sending it to the power amplifier. Microphones that yield similar results often cost a lot more.

9. MAINTENANCE

A piano needs less maintenance than most other instruments. All you really need to do is to keep it clean and make sure that the humidity and temperature in your home don't cause problems.

There are many things you'd best leave to professionals, from moving the instrument to tuning, regulating, and even some of the cleaning. Chapter 10 tells you all about it.

High-gloss or satin
Instruments with a high-gloss or satin finish are easily kept clean with a soft, lint-free cloth. Wipe in long, straight lines rather than in circles, and exert as little pressure as possible: Strange though it may sound, dust can scratch. You may begin by using a very slightly damp cloth, to pick up the dust. Most fresh fingerprints can be removed by first breathing on them, so that the lacquer mists over.

French-polished or waxed
On French-polished pianos or instruments treated with wax, a soft, dry cloth will usually do, provided the instrument is cleaned regularly. If it needs more work, ask an expert.

Cleaners
Special cleaners are available for every type of finish, costing ten to fifteen dollars a bottle. That doesn't sound cheap, but you may only use it once a year, so it'll last a long time. The instructions that come with the cleaner tell you which finishes it is suitable for. Some piano cleaners have an anti-static (dust repellent) effect.

Household cleaners
Don't use household cleaners on pianos; they're often too abrasive, they may leave a residue or even damage the finish. Always avoid using silicone based cleaners, as they may damage the action.

Soap
To remove marks on high-gloss and satin lacquer finishes you can moisten a soft cloth with a mild soap solution (mild cleaning liquid or shampoo).

Polishing polyester
Those very fine scratches that can quickly show up in polyester finishes can be removed with special polishing agents – but if you want to stay on the safe side, let your technician take care of this. Before using any kind of polishing liquid, always dust off the instrument. Deeper scratches or dents can be filled. If you want an invisible repair it's best, again, to get a technician to do it.

French polish
A French-polished finish can also be treated by very lightly buffing it. Ask a piano dealer for the right cleaner. Any damage should be repaired by a professional. Getting an old instrument French-polished again costs thousands of dollars.

Wax
If you have a piano finished with wax, or a satin-finish instrument whose lacquer has worn thin, you can treat it very lightly with beeswax once a year. Experts advise against using a wax that contains silicones. Never use wax on pianos with a synthetic outer ply (see page 32).

Keys
Clean the keys with a slightly damp cloth, moving from the back to the front of the keys rather than sideways. If the keys are plastic-covered, you may spray a very small amount of glass cleaner onto the cloth – not onto the keys themselves – or use a special key cleaner. Always dry the keys immediately after cleaning them. The color of ebonized black keys can sometimes rub off. If so, don't use the same cloth to clean the white keys.

The sides

Now and again, clean the sides of the keys too, as they get dirty when you play the neighboring keys.

The sides of the keys get dirty too.

Ivory

Don't use glass cleaners or other cleaners on ivory-covered keys, and dry them off at once: Ivory is sensitive to moisture. Another tip: Only use cloths that can't leave a stain on the keys.

The inside?

The inside of the piano is best left to a piano technician. If you want to clean it yourself, please limit yourself to using a vacuum cleaner to get rid of the dust that gathers at the bottom of an upright. Take off the lower panel, which is usually attached only with a simple clamp. Don't touch the strings or any parts of the action and the pedal work with any part of the vacuum cleaner, and always use a soft, long-haired brush attachment.

Grand piano

Dust under the frame of a grand piano is very hard to get rid of, so better leave this to a technician too. Never use a hair dryer to blow the dust away: The heat may damage the soundboard, and the dust will usually settle somewhere else in the instrument. Dust on the tops of the dampers of a grand piano can be carefully removed with a feather duster.

Moths

The anti-moth treatment the felt receives in the factory eventually vanishes. Keeping the instrument dust-free helps to keep moths away. If moths are already a problem or you think they might be, you may hang a piece of odor-free moth paper on the inside of the upper frame. Technicians can do this for you too.

Woodworm

Playing your instrument helps prevent woodworm, as these animals don't like vibrating wood. If a lot of tiny holes and tunnels are visible, call an expert.

Questions

When you buy an instrument in a store, you will often be told what maintenance is required. You can also ask your technician if you have any questions. There is space to list them on page 135.

PREVENTION

You can avoid a lot of cleaning, polishing, and repairs by these tips.

Keep it closed

Close the lid and the fallboard when you are not playing, to prevent dust from settling in the action and the windings of the bass strings. Wood-finished instruments may discolor unevenly if the fallboard is always open: The wood will keep its original color only where the fallboard rests against the upper panel. Direct sunlight – which should be avoided at all times – will speed up any discoloration.

Clean hands

Washing your hands before playing helps keeping the keys clean. Handling the fallboard and lids by the bottom edge or sides as much as possible helps to avoid visible fingerprints on the instrument.

No flowers, plants, or drinks

Don't put flowers or plants on the instrument. Many parts inside are sensitive to moisture, and the outside often is too. French-polish is especially vulnerable. For the same reason, don't put drinks on the cabinet or on the *key blocks* or *end blocks* (the small flat areas at either end of the keyboard).

Scratches
If you do put photo frames, lamps, or anything else on the instrument, make sure there's felt underneath. Even music books scratch most finishes, eventually.

Candles
Spilled candle-wax is difficult to remove without damaging the finish, and it's especially annoying if it ends up between the keys – so keep candles away from the instrument.

Strings and felt
Avoid touching the strings or felt parts because your natural skin oil and the acids it contains are not good for them: Felt gets greasy and strings rust.

Cover
If you really want to protect your investment, consider buying a cover. They are available for both grand pianos and uprights, completely covering the instrument.

Moving
At some time you may want to shift your piano within your house or apartment. If you are in any doubt, leave this to professional piano movers (see page 98), especially if you are planning to move it to another room. This will help prevent damage to your instrument, your house, and yourself.

DRY AND MOIST, HOT AND COLD
In many houses, the humidity and temperature are so steady that a piano can happily grow old there. But if conditions are really dry or humid, if the humidity changes fast and often, or if the room temperature in the room is very low for some time, you can get all kinds of problems. The soundboard can crack, panels can warp, keys can stick and tuning pins come loose… Fortunately, all of these developments are preventable.

Dry

If it's freezing outside and the heating is on indoors, the air gets drier and drier, with most heating systems. As your lips chap, wood will contract. If the soundboard contracts, the crown (page 60) gets lower, which reduces the tension on the strings. Tip: Air conditioning systems also make the humidity level drop.

Moist

In summer, the air is at its most moist. In humid conditions, wood expands. That means the tension on the soundboard increases, and with it the tension on the strings. If it gets really humid, keys can stick, just like doors, drawers and windows. All kinds of other parts can suffer from moisture: Damp hammer heads produce a squidgy sound, the action may get noticeably heavier, and strings can rust. Old houses with gas fires are usually quite damp.

Forty to sixty

Many experts say the best humidity level for pianos – and for people, luckily – is between 40% and 60%, although other figures are sometimes quoted. It needn't matter if the humidity briefly goes outside of that range, but if it lasts for days you may have problems.

Changes

It's at least as important that the humidity doesn't change too fast. You should take that into account if you move an instrument from an old house with a gas fire to a much drier apartment with central heating and air conditioning – or the other way around.

Hygrometer

You can measure humidity using a *hygrometer*, on sale from all piano stores. The cheapest models, which cost around twenty dollars, have a dial and a pointer. Digital hygrometers are more expensive, but they're usually more accurate and often include a thermometer.

Calibrating

There is another difference. A dial-type hygrometer, which uses a hair to measure the humidity level, gets sluggish and becomes steadily less responsive. However, if you leave it outside for a night, the moist air will refresh it for a whole year. Better still, you can recalibrate it yourself. Around the time of year when the weather gets colder and you switch the heating back on, wrap it in a wet cloth for a quarter of an hour and immediately afterwards set the pointer to 98%.

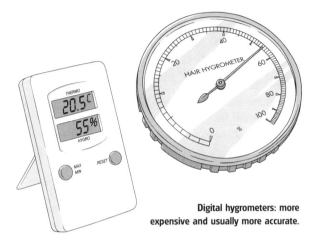

Digital hygrometers: more expensive and usually more accurate.

Sunlight and heating
Wood heats up and dries out if you leave it too close to a heater, and putting a piano above a heating vent is asking for trouble. Direct sunlight is just as bad, certainly if it shines straight onto the soundboard of the instrument. Finishes can be easily damaged by direct sunlight too.

Temperature
Pianos are like people when it comes to temperature as well. Around 65–70°F (18–21°C) is ideal. Temperatures lower than 60°F (16°C) may cause problems, so it's advisable to keep the heating on in the winter, even if you're not there. The more steady the temperature and humidity, the more stable the tuning of the instrument will be.

Extra measures
Whether you need to take extra measures to keep the humidity at the right level depends on a lot of things. For instance, houseplants and an open kitchen cause extra moisture in the air, whereas a very well-stocked bookcase helps to keep the humidity a little more constant. To keep

things constant, an upright piano is better off standing near an inner wall than a thin outer wall.

Too dry?

Really, the biggest problem is excessively dry air, and the worst times are when it's freezing outside. There are steps you can take to avoid dry air. If you have radiators and the humidity falls suddenly, a stopgap solution is to hang some damp towels over them. This is effective, but not very stylish. You can also stick a rolled-up newspaper into a container half-full of water and stand it in the bottom of an upright piano. The newspaper helps the water to evaporate, but this will take a long while. What's more, it may go moldy, the moisture may cause rust, the whole thing could fall over or – more likely still – simply be forgotten.

Internal climate control

As an alternative, there are internal climate control systems that keep the humidity level inside the instrument stable. Advanced systems work automatically: If it's too dry, the built-in hygrostat automatically switches on the moisturizer; if the air is too damp, a drying unit is activated. A warning light comes on when you need to refill the tank with water, which is easy to do with a special tube. Including installation, such systems cost around three to six hundred dollars. Damp-Chaser is the best-known name.

Other systems

There are many other internal systems, which range from very basic and affordable water-filled tubes to more advanced humidifiers, hygrostats, and heating elements. They differ in price, of course, and also in the maintenance they require.

The whole room

There are also various types of devices that humidify the whole room. This extends the benefits of a better climate to you and to your furniture, for instance. Each system has its own advantages and drawbacks. Some of the more common are listed below.

Hot and cold systems

Steam humidifiers are available from around seventy-five

or a hundred dollars. They work fast and generate some extra heat, which some people find much too damp. What's more, you can hear some models bubbling away when they're switched on. Cold humidifier systems are quieter, but more expensive. They take longer to work, and they need quite a lot of maintenance (cleaning, filling, and so on); some systems require additives for the water. Some are also capable of drying the air during humid periods. Depending on how your house is heated, it may also be a good idea to have a central humidifier installed.

Look and compare

A few tips: Visit a few different stores and ask about these and other systems, compare prices and energy consumption, ask whether you need any extras and what they cost, and consider the maximum volume of air each device can handle. Larger rooms may need two. You can buy them from stores that sell household appliances as well as from piano stores.

10. TRANSPORTATION, TUNING AND REGULATION

Most pianos need to be tuned two or three times a year if they are to sound their best. If you want to get as much enjoyment as possible from your instrument for as long as possible, it will also need regulating every few years. New strings, new hammers, and many other new parts can be fitted in due course if required. All of those jobs are best left to the professionals – as is transportation.

It's best to use an established firm of piano movers to move your instrument. If you are buying from a store, delivery is usually included in the price; if you are buying from a private owner or renting, it usually isn't.

Costs

The costs vary between roughly a hundred and four hundred dollars, excluding a mileage charge. The exact price may also depend on the size of the instrument. Other additional charges may be for stair steps, using a crane, or anything else that makes the job harder. Always ask for a binding quote in advance – but you will only get one when the movers know exactly what the job involves.

Indoors

Even if a piano only has to be moved from one room to another, it's a good idea to get professionals to do the job.

Specialized

You'll find specialized piano movers in the *Yellow Pages* or through piano stores. Tip: Check if the movers are insured for any damage they may cause.

Space

Check beforehand whether the instrument will fit where you want to take it, and don't forget to look at the dimensions of doors or windows, staircases, and other relevant obstacles. Some movers may even come and take a look themselves.

Damage

If the instrument being moved is secondhand, always take a look at it together with one of the movers and list any scratches and other damage. This helps to avoid disputes about damage being caused during transportation.

TUNING

A guitar or a violin has to be tuned every time it is played. A piano doesn't. Two or three times a year is often enough.

Out of tune

Every piano goes out of tune eventually, even if it hasn't been played, one reason being that the tension of the strings varies with changes in humidity and temperature (see page 93 and onwards). The more stable those two factors are, the more stable the tuning of the instrument will be. Tuning stability depends on the instrument itself too: Better instruments often detune less than cheaper ones.

Piano tuners and technicians

Tuning a piano is a job for a professional, from the 'setting' of the tuning pins to the precise tuning of over two hundred strings to each other. Many piano tuners are also piano technicians, so they do repairs and adjustments too.

Certified technicians

Every country has one or more organizations of certified piano tuners and technicians, where you can apply for member addresses (please see pages 132–133 for details). Of course, not every technician wants to be a member of such an organization, so good piano technicians can be found elsewhere too. Ask other piano owners whether they know a good tuner, or let a piano salesperson advise you.

Tuning: a job for an expert.

How much

A normal tuning takes an hour to an hour and a half. The price may vary from sixty to over a hundred dollars, depending on where you live, the proficiency or the reputation of the tuner, and other factors. Many tuners charge seventy-five to eighty-five dollars.

How often

If you play about five to ten hours a week, it's usually enough to have your instrument tuned two to three times a year. If an instrument needs to be tuned more often or if it goes out of tune very quickly, something is wrong with it, or with the conditions in the room, or with the tuner: One thing that sets good tuners aside is that they provide the instrument with a stable tuning.

When

Because temperature and humidity affect the piano's tuning, it's usually considered best to have your piano tuned in the spring and in the fall.

More often

New and recently re-strung instruments need to be tuned

more often, one reason being that new strings will stretch some more before they reach a stable length. Some tuners say that one extra tuning per year for the first few years is enough, others prefer to give a piano two extra tunings in the first year. The particular instrument plays a role in the decision too.

Too late

If you can clearly hear that a piano is out of tune, you're really too late in getting it tuned. The more a tuner has to adjust it, the harder it is to produce a stable tuning. What's more, more turning of the tuning pins causes more wear to the pinblock.

Pitch drops

Some pianos never seem to go out of tune. Should you still have them tuned regularly? Yes, because they *do* go out of tune, but it happens so slowly that you may get used to it – which doesn't help developing a good ear for pitches. If a piano is not being tuned, the pitch will drop over the years, the bass section usually a little less than the other octaves.

Too low

Some pianos may still sound in tune, even if the pitch has dropped. Then too, tuning is necessary. A piano that sounds too low can't be used with other instruments (unless you can tune them down to the piano), and it won't sound as good as it can: Pianos are designed to sound at A=440 (see page 68). And of course, the further the tuning has dropped, the harder it can be to bring the instrument back to the right pitch, even with a *double tuning*.

Just moved

If a piano has just been moved, it often needs to get used to its new environment for two or three weeks – and there's a fair chance that it will suddenly go out of tune or not play as well in that time. Don't call a piano technician until those few weeks have passed. Only then are tuning and regulating useful.

Also, those few weeks may allow you to discover that the instrument needs additional voicing to match its sound to the acoustics of the room.

Electronic tuner?

There are electronic tuning devices for pianos, but they don't replace a technician. Technicians may use one as an aid, but it'll never replace their ears. Also, there are books that promise to teach you to tune your piano yourself – but no book can substitute the knowledge and experience of a good technician.

EQUAL TEMPERAMENT

A piano is difficult to tune because it has so many strings, but that's not all. The following section explains some of the backgrounds of piano tuning, and tells you why two tuners will always tune an instrument slightly differently. If you don't like a little musical math, skip ahead to page 104.

Twice as fast

The A that most instruments are tuned to is slightly to the right of the center of a piano keyboard: the A4. At that pitch, the strings vibrate at a speed of 440 vibrations per second (440 hertz). Eight white keys or an octave higher, at A5, the strings vibrate twice as fast (880 hertz).

One and a half

In a similar way, there are specific ratios for the other intervals. For example, if you go up a fifth (five white keys, *e.g.*, C4 to G4), the strings at that key will vibrate one and a half times as fast.

Problem

Now, there is a slight problem, one that experts have wrestled with for centuries. In the illustration on the following page you'll see what it is: The different ratios don't match. The calculation shown above the keyboard fixes the note A4 at a different pitch (880Hz) from the one shown below the keyboard (891Hz).

Hiding

The solution? The tuner 'hides' these discrepancies by tuning most of the notes a tiny bit too high or too low. The differences are so small that you can't hear them, or only just. For instance, C4 is tuned to around 262 hertz, rather than 264.

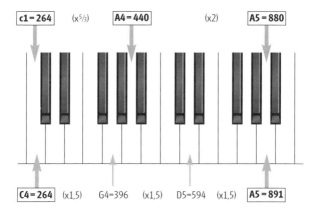

The sums don't add up...

The solution

So tuners have to decide how much they allow certain notes to deviate. They do so by listening to the beats.

Beats

If you play C4 and G4 together on a properly tuned piano, you'll hear very soft 'waves' in the sound. These are called beats. If you then play C4 and A4, you'll hear faster beats. The beats betray the fact that even a well-tuned piano is slightly 'out of tune': If it were perfectly tuned, you wouldn't hear any *beats*.

Equal temperament

On a piano, nearly every combination of two notes will produce beats, however slightly. In other words: The discrepancies (the mathematical errors, so to speak) are equally spread across the whole keyboard. This is known as *equal temperament* or the *well-tempered scale*.

Differently in tune

By listening very closely to these beats, the tuner knows how much too low or too high each note needs to be tuned. Exactly which frequencies he chooses to achieve a balanced tuning depends on the individual tuner. That means that a different tuner may make your piano sound just slightly different – not out of tune, just 'differently in tune.' Of course, you may prefer one tuning – and thus, one tuner – to another.

Meantone tuning   Tipcode PIANO-018

It is possible to tune a piano perfectly and without hearing any beats, but such a *meantone tuning*, which was used before equal temperament was introduced, has its limitations. If you tune a piano this way, it can only sound in tune in certain keys. Tune it so C major sounds perfect, and it will sound awful in B-major, F-minor, and other keys. Equal temperament offers the solution. It makes it possible to tune a piano so that it can be used in all key signatures.

REGULATING AND VOICING

The more you play and the older the instrument is, the more servicing it will usually require. On the other hand, your piano will need less frequent maintenance if you keep the lid and fallboard closed when you are not playing it; if your technician does some minor maintenance and checks the regulation and voicing as well as the tuning; or if you play for only a few hours a week. The quality and the condition of the instrument also play a role. A good technician will help you keep an eye on all of those things. If something goes wrong in the meantime, from breaking strings to sticking keys or creaking pedals, call an expert at once.

Regulating

Every instrument needs to be regulated periodically. This means adjusting the action and the pedals and everything that's connected to them, so the piano plays the way it should, providing a uniform response along the entire keyboard, control over the tone and the dynamics, and allowing you to play anything you want – or can.

Voicing

Over the years, the felt of the hammer heads gets gradually denser and harder, which makes the tone steadily thinner and edgier. That's why every instrument needs to be voiced sooner or later (see also page 51). Hammers can be reshaped if they have become flattened, or if the strings have worn deep grooves into them – provided there is still enough felt left and it is in good condition. Hammers can be softened by inserting *voicing needles*, or they can be hardened in different ways. Rather than improving a piano's performance, voicing can also be required to adjust the tone of the instrument to your liking or to the room's acoustics.

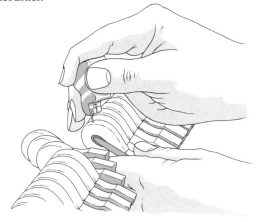

Making hammer heads softer by pricking them.

Reconditioning

As the parts of the piano are exposed to wear, temperature and humidity changes, and aging, there will come a time that tuning, regulating, and voicing aren't sufficient any more to make your instrument sound good and play well. By that time, major servicing, generally indicated as *reconditioning*, is necessary. What exactly needs to be done depends on the age and the condition of the instrument, among other things.

Rebuilding

If major parts (strings, pinblock, action, etc.) have to be renewed, technicians speak of (partially) *rebuilding* the instrument. This may make it as good as it was when new – or even better. Of course, the instrument should be worth the cost of such an operation.

11. BACK IN TIME

The action in today's grand pianos in not that much different from the one Bartolomeo Cristofori built some three hundred years ago. Even so, there have been plenty of developments since his day – and of course, much went on before too.

As early as the fourteenth century, and perhaps even before, there was an instrument with keys and strings: the *clavichord* (*clavis* means key, *chord* means string). When played, small brass wedges made the strings vibrate very softly.

Plucking
The harpsichord, which was most popular in the seventeenth and eighteenth centuries, sounded a lot bigger and fuller than the clavichord. Harpsichord strings were originally plucked by the quills of raven feathers, which were attached to the ends of the keys.

Spinet
A *spinet* works like a harpsichord, but it is a size smaller, and the strings run at an angle backwards from the keys. On a *virginal*, another variant, the strings usually run perpendicular to the keys, from left to right.

Touch-sensitive
Harpsichords, spinets, and virginals are not touch-sensitive: Every note sounds equally loud, no matter how the keys are struck. This was a problem the Italian harpsichord maker Bartolomeo Cristofori (1655-1731) set out to solve.

Around 1700 he began building an instrument which would be able to sound both loud and soft, based on the harpsichord but using hammers instead of raven quills.

Piano e forte

The result, which he unveiled a few years later, he christened the *gravicembalo col piano e forte*, literally meaning 'harpsichord with loud and soft.' A good quarter of a century after his first experiments, Cristofori came up with an improved action, which was very similar to the present system.

Pianoforte, fortepiano

The full name of the instrument was soon shortened to *pianoforte* or *fortepiano*. Just like harpsichords and spinets, these forerunners of the modern piano are still used to play the music of that era. The main difference is that the tone of a pianoforte or *hammerklavier*, produced by leather-clad hammers, is often described as more transparent, brighter, and shorter than that of a modern grand piano.

The oldest preserved piano, a Cristofori, built in 1720, with a range of four-and-a-half octaves, no pedals, and two-string unisons for each note.

Square piano

From about 1750 to 1850, the *square piano* or *square grand* was very popular. Its horizontal strings ran from left to right through a rectangular cabinet.

A square piano with over five octaves and a lyre with three pedals (Pleyel, 1816).

Vertical

The first upright pianos were built midway through the eighteenth century. Names like *giraffe piano* and *pyramid piano* indicate that such instruments came in all kinds of shapes and sizes. The precursor of the modern upright piano appeared around 1800. Matthias Müller, Isaac Hawkins, and Robert Wornum are the three names most often mentioned in its development.

Inventions

Since Cristofori, a whole lot of things have been changed, invented, and improved. For instance, in 1821 the Frenchman Sebastian Érard devised the *double escapement* mechanism or *repetition mechanism*, the system that allows the greater repetition speed of a grand piano. Before that, Érard had already introduced the agraffes and other innovations. His compatriot Henri Pape was also responsible for countless inventions, from felt hammer heads to the cross-strung upright piano. Steinway, a manufacturer which would acquire more than a hundred patents, produced the first cross-strung grands midway through the nineteenth century.

Louder

Larger concert halls meant that pianos had to produce more volume and a bigger sound, so ever-heavier gauge strings were introduced over the years. In turn, those strings needed bigger hammer heads to set them in motion, and the increased string tension required a cast-iron frame, which the American piano maker Alpheus Babcock patented in 1825. The soundboard also became steadily thicker, and the number of octaves grew from four and a half to more than seven.

Player piano

A very different invention, dating back to the end of the nineteenth century, is the *player piano* – a piano that works

An English piano built around 1800 (Robert Knight, London; Cristofori collection, Amsterdam).

much like a barrel organ, which has paper rolls punched with holes which tell the mechanism when to play each note. These days, player pianos use digital technology (see Chapter 7).

A hundred years

Little has changed in the last hundred years or so, but of course piano makers have not been idle. The results of their efforts range from using synthetic components to player grands with built-in CD players, and from various systems to make uprights repeat faster, to special cabinet designs, and to smaller-sized keyboards to fit children's hands.

Only a few

Then there are lots of other models of which only a few are ever built – Plexiglas grands, for example, or pianos with a glass soundboard, instruments with eight extra keys per octave so that you can play quarter-tones too, or double grands with two keyboards and two soundboards, or even instruments for left-handed pianists, with the bass notes on the right…

12. THE FAMILY

Pianos are referred to as string instruments, but also as percussion instruments, because the strings are struck by hammers – and they're known as keyboard instruments too. This chapter introduces you to some of the relatives of that part of the family.

Basically, pianos belong to the family of string instruments, like guitars and violins. Within that family they fall under the category of keyboard instruments, as do the harpsichord, the spinet, and the fortepiano mentioned in the previous chapter. In this chapter you'll find descriptions of some other keyboard instruments. The digital piano, which appeared in the early 1980s, was discussed in Chapter 7.

With hammers
The only family member without keys in this chapter is the *hammered dulcimer*. The strings of this instrument are sounded by striking them with hammers, just like a piano's. The difference is that you hold the hammers yourself. You are most likely to see the dulcimer, which is also known as *cymbalo* or *cymbalom*, in gypsy orchestras.

With metal plates
A *celesta* or *celeste* looks like a small piano but is actually a glockenspiel with keys; the hammers strike metal plates which produce a ringing tone. The sound is very soft, and the instrument is scarcely used outside of classical music.

With reeds
Most *accordions* have a regular keyboard for the right hand;

the bass notes are played by the left hand on a bank of round, black buttons. When you stretch or squeeze the bellows, air flows past metal reeds, making them vibrate – just like in a mouth organ.

With forks

The *electric piano* is a forerunner of the digital piano. Instead of strings, most electric pianos have metal forks, tongues, or rods, which are struck by hammers. The vibrations are picked up by one or more magnetic pickups (like on an electric guitar), and from there are sent to the amplifier. Electric pianos are no longer produced, but some classic instruments, such as the Fender Rhodes, are still in use.

With pipes

An organ may look like a piano, but it is actually a very different instrument, which is played very differently too. One major difference is that where a piano note decays after a while, an organ will sound until you let go of the key. This is just one reason why organs require a different playing technique. On classical or church organs, air is blown through a large number of pipes. Naturally, that produces a very different sound to a set of piano strings. Another difference is that organs are not touch-sensitive, but most of them do have a volume pedal.

With electronics

You'll always find a volume pedal on an electronic organ, which, like most bigger organs, also has a *pedalboard*: an oversized keyboard that you operate with your left foot.

With tonewheels

Just like electric pianos, there are famous types of organs which are still favored by some musicians, even though they're no longer in production. The best-known example is the Hammond organ, especially their B-3. This so-called *tonewheel organ* has been emulated by several digital instruments or modules.

With samples

Home keyboards were developed from the organ. Apart from a number of organ sounds, home keyboards have dozens or hundreds of other sounds, from guitars and strings to complete drum sets, clarinets, rain showers, gunshots, and helicopters. All of those sounds have been sampled, just like in a sound module (see page 77). Keyboards also come with a standard automatic accompaniment feature: Play a chord, choose a tempo, and you hear a complete accompanying orchestra – so all you have to do is play the melody or a solo.

A keyboard: hundreds of sounds, automatic accompaniment, a recorder, built-in amplification, and much more.

Piano?

Most home keyboards also offer a choice of piano sounds. Even so, you can't really 'play the piano' on this instrument, for one thing because most home keyboards don't have a weighted action (see page 82).

Synthesizer

To synthesize means to produce or combine artificially. With a synthesizer you can make your own sounds. The instrument usually has a number of basic sounds which you can edit in all kinds of ways – digitally, acoustically, or both – to create new sounds. There are software synths too, which allow you to use your computer as a musical instrument.

More and more alike

The differences between instruments like synthesizers, keyboards, and digital pianos are getting ever smaller: You can buy digital pianos with home keyboard options, there are home keyboards with synthesizer options, and synthesizers with weighted keys. *Tipbook Keyboard and Digital Piano* (see page 138) takes a closer look at all of those digital instruments, and also at workstations, samplers, and other instruments and equipment.

13. HOW THEY'RE MADE

Some piano factories build their instruments one by one; others have mass production lines. Some factories produce thirty pianos per year, others thirty thousand, or even more. Of course, there are many other differences between one factory and the next. Generally speaking, though, pianos are built in the way described below.

Tipcode PIANO-019

Building a piano takes time to do properly. A top model can easily take more than two years to craft, from the moment the first planks are sawn to the final tuning and voicing. The wood used for expensive instruments has often been dried and cured for five or even ten years.

Soundboard

Most soundboards are made of solid spruce planks about four inches (10 cm) wide. The ribs are glued at right angles to the grain of the soundboard. A press may be used to create the crown, among other techniques. On the other side of the soundboard are the bridges over which the strings will run.

Frame

The frame is made in a special foundry, and then filed, sanded smooth, drilled, and finished. The holes for the two-hundred-plus tuning pins must be drilled in exactly the right places.

Strings

Like the frame, the steel strings are almost always purchased from an outside supplier. The only part of string manufacture that piano factories often do themselves is the winding of the bass strings – by hand, even.

First tuning

Once the pinblock is in place, the strings are stretched over the soundboard and tuned for the first time. Since there are no hammers yet, the tuner plucks the strings as a guitarist would. This process is called *chipping*. After tuning, the entire structure – consisting of the frame with back posts, soundboard, strings, and pinblock – is given time to settle. The strings, now under tension, are able to stretch until they reach a fairly stable length.

The cabinet

Meanwhile, in a different part of the factory, the cabinet is being manufactured. Curved wooden parts, like some fallboards or the rim of a grand piano, are usually bent into shape using large presses or numerous clamps.

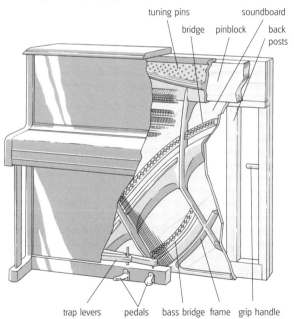

The cabinet, the back posts, and the rest.

Finishing

Finishing the wooden case usually involves many steps, including staining, filling, sanding, and polishing.

Sawing the keyboard

The keyboard is sawn from a large piece of laminated wood, somewhat like a giant jigsaw puzzle. The sharps – small black plastic or wooden bars – are glued on afterwards.

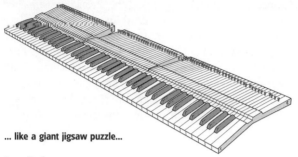

... like a giant jigsaw puzzle...

Installed

Once the frame, soundboard, and strings have been installed in the cabinet, the action, the keyboard, and the pedals are fitted.

Regulation

The regulation of the instrument takes a lot of time, if done properly. For example, all the keys must be perfectly balanced, so weights are used to determine how much lead, if any, needs to be added to each key. In addition, each key must be exactly level with all the others, and the key dip should be the same for every key. All the dampers must respond equally quickly. And so must all the hammers, all the let-off buttons, all the pilots, all the repetition springs, all the whippen-top flanges...

Voicing and tuning

Proper voicing is a time-consuming business too, mainly consisting of giving the hammers the desired hardness by inserting needles in the felt. Often instruments will be voiced more than once, just as they are tuned and regulated several times. Higher-quality instruments are often broken in by machines that play them for many hours before they leave the factory.

14. BRANDS

There are hundreds of piano brands, with names old and new. Famous names, obscure names, family names and made-up names. This chapter offers a short introduction to the main piano brands and brand names[1], and sheds some light on a very complex market.

In the first half of the twentieth century there were many, many piano factories in the USA and Europe – hundreds of them, mostly rather small, each with its own brand name. Today, only a few of those companies still exist. Most have vanished, and a few ever-larger factories, mainly in Asia, build instruments under a wide variety of brand names – often using names of the old companies.

One makes, many brands

One Asian piano manufacturer may make pianos under a dozen or more different brand names, as well as a trade name of their own. Conversely, there are piano brands that have been made in at least four different factories within a twenty-year time span.

Confusing

This is just a minor indication of how complex the piano market is. You can buy a piano with a reputable brand name today, and find out that the name had been sold to a not-so-reputable maker not long before. Buying your instrument at a reputable dealer is the best way to make

[1] Trademarks and/or usernames have been used in this book solely to identify the products or instruments discussed. Such use does not identify endorsement by or affiliation with the trademark owner(s).

sure you buy a good instrument, backed by a proper warranty. Also, stock yourself with up-to-date information via the Internet, magazines, and other sources (see pages 131–132). The following is merely an indication of the brands you may come across, and it's by no means intended to be complete.

Germany

The piano is an Italian invention, and many of the first improvements came from France and England. Even so, German manufacturers soon built up the most impressive reputation – and many companies all over the world advertise their use of German parts for their instruments, from Kluge keyboards to Abel hammer heads. German pianos do not come cheap, often starting around seven or eight thousand dollars.

Names

The image of German pianos explains why German-sounding names are often used on pianos – just as Asian-built steel-string guitars often have American names. Names of famous composers are also very popular; Schubert, Strauss, Schumann, and Wagner are just some examples. These brand names, of course, don't offer any information about the quality of the instrument.

Countries

Knowing the country an instrument comes from may be of little help too. For instance, you can buy Chinese pianos with European parts, and European pianos with Chinese parts are just as common. Also, there are 'Japanese' pianos which are completely assembled in Europe or America (like cars), and American companies that have part or all of their instruments made in Asia. Finally, piano makers in the former Soviet Union and China are getting better too, even though these countries may not yet have strong reputations for building the instrument.

Image, price, and quality

A country's reputation for building pianos is often reflected by the prices charged for those instruments. Germany has a great reputation. Of course they do, you could say: the Germans make rather expensive pianos only. Other countries, making less expensive instruments only, have a less favorable reputation. The bottom line? The quality of an instrument is not necessarily related to its origins, but rather to its price. Expensive pianos are usually a lot better than cheap ones. Just like cars…

House and stencil brands

Not all makes are for sale in all piano stores. For instance, some brands are distributed through only a limited number of dealers. Then there are the so-called *house brands* or *stencil brand*s: Piano stores, importers, and distributors can simply order a number of pianos and have their own brand name put on them.

Standard models

If the instruments have certain features consciously chosen by the dealer, they may be referred to as a house brand; if they are a standard model, only the brand name being different, they're often called *stencil pianos*. A tip: Identical instruments which are sold under different brand names can have very different prices.

The brands

There are only a limited number of brands that you'll find in most stores. Some of the best-known are described very briefly below. Others are covered later in this chapter, divided by country. The information shown may become out-of-date: A brand currently being built in Europe may, in a few years, be imported from Asia, or the other way around, for instance. There are brands you won't find here – which doesn't necessarily mean they're not good instruments – and some brands that are mentioned may not be available anymore, or not where you live.

Baldwin® Baldwin is one the main names in the American piano industry. The first Baldwin pianos were made in the 1890s. The company also produces Wurlitzer and Chickering, and imports the Chinese made Kranich & Bach pianos.

 Bechstein (1853) is the oldest and most expensive of the three brands produced by the

Zimmermann® German Bechstein Gruppe. The two others, W. Hoffmann (1904) and Zimmermann (1884), joined this group in the early 1990s.

Bohemia® Bohemia is one of the better-known Czech names. Schlögl and SCHLÖGL® Rieger-Kloss belong to the same company, which has been around since 1871. Two related brands are Fibich and Hofmann & Czerny.

KAWAI® Kawai (1927), one of Japan's largest piano makers, also builds digital pianos and acoustic instruments for other makes in the lower-middle to higher-middle price range. Boston (marketed by Steinway) is one of the better-known examples.

PETROF® Petrof (1864), the Czech brand made in Europe's largest piano factory, produces uprights and grands in virtually all sizes. Scholze, Förster, and Rösler are three separate factories which form part of the Petrof group.

PLEYEL® Pleyel was founded in 1807 by the French composer Ignace Pleyel. Pleyel is the highest priced brand of the company which also produces Gaveau, Rameau, and Érard. Schulmann is a cheaper, Asian-made Pleyel brand.

samick® One of the biggest companies in the music industry, Samick (Korea) makes pianos and guitars in Korea, the US, and other countries, under their own trade name as well as for many other companies.

SAUTER® Besides 'classical' models, the German company Sauter (1819) makes various modern uprights in striking designs with matching benches.

SCHIMMEL® Schimmel (1885) is one of the largest European manufacturers. As well as building classic models, this German firm has always been a leading innovator.

SEILER® Edward Seiler started his company in 1849, and like quite a few other German brands, the company has been run by the descendants of the founder for many generations.

YAMAHA® The one-man organ factory started by Torakusu Yamaha in 1889 is now one of the world's largest builders of musical instruments. The Japanese company is also known for many other products, from motorbikes to hi-fi equipment.

YOUNG ⓒ CHANG® Young Chang (Korea) is one of the many Asian companies in which German experts play an important role. Besides its own uprights and grands, the factory builds or used to build instruments for US and other brands.

High-end instruments

Of course, this section of well-known brands would not be complete without two of the most prestigious names in the industry: Bösendorfer and Steinway. Both brands make instruments in the very highest price range only.

Bösendorfer® Bösendorfer was founded in 1828 in Vienna, where the factory is still located (on a street called Bösendorfer-strasse…).

STEINWAY & SONS® Steinway has two facto-ries: one in Hamburg, Germany (the original home of the family, then called Steinweg) and one in America, where Steinway & Sons was founded in 1853.

Made in the US

Mason & Hamlin has built pianos in the US for around 150 years. **Story & Clark**, another US brand with a history of a century and a half, has a very limited US production, with some of its models coming from Asia. **Charles R. Walter** and **Janssen** are two young brands of the same company. **Astin-Weight** started making their unique instruments in the late 1950s. **Fandrich & Sons** built their Fandrich Vertical Action in Asian-made upright pianos.

Formerly made in the US

Many brands that used to be made in the US now come from Asian factories. Some examples are **Kohler & Campbell**, **Krakauer**, **Everett**, **George Steck**, **Weber**, and **Wm. Knabe** and **Knab**e, two brand names from the American company that is known for QuietTime and PianoDisc (see Chapter 7).

Old brand names

A few examples of better known US companies that have disappeared (but they may return in the market, in due time…) are **Aeolian**, a company that in little under a hundred years was involved in at least twenty piano brands; **Kimball**, owner of Bösendorfer (see above), having made pianos for a little over hundred years; and **Falcone** and **Sohmer**, both discontinued in 1994.

China

The largest Chinese piano maker is Guangzhou Piano Manufactory in China, with its own brand **Pearl River.** The company has a joint venture with Yamaha and also makes or has made instruments under a wide variety of other brand names. Some other makers are the Beijing Piano Company, the Dongbei Piano Company, the Shanghai Piano Company, and the Yantai Longfeng Piano Company, which sells its instruments under various brand names. Three examples are **Nordiska**, **Carl Ebel,** and **Richter**, all brands from European origins.

Germany

There are numerous other German brands besides the names listed above. Some well-known examples are **Blüthner**, featuring aliquot strings in the high treble of its grand pianos; **Grotrian**, also in the high price range; **Ibach** (1794), the oldest surviving piano company, which at one time had instruments made in Korea; **August Förster**, operating in a noticeably higher price range than its Czech namesake (see Petrof); **Pfeiffer**, which also supplies **Hupfeld** and **Rönisch** instruments; **Feurich**, run by Julius Feurich (the fifth generation); **Wilh. Steinberg**, a medium-sized factory which, among its other models, produces Germany's most affordable upright; and **Steingraeber**, where you can have pianos custom made.

The brands **Brückner** and **Steinmann** also come from Germany. Blüthner produces mid-priced instruments under the name **Haessler**.

Britain
One of the best-known British names is **Kemble**, established in 1911. **Whelpdale**, founded in 1876 as an importer for Blüthner, supplies the smaller brands **Knight**, **Bentley**, **Welmar**, **Marshal & Rose**, and **Broadwood**, among others. **Woodchester** is a very young company (1994), established in the former Bentley factory.

Poland
Even though it's no longer in production, **Th. Betting** is one of the most famous Polish brand names. Theodor Betting, founder of the company, also established the Polish firm **Schirmer & Sons**. Other brands with Polish origins include **Fibiger**, **Calisia**, **Ravenstein**, and **Steinbeck**. In addition, many parts for other manufacturers are made in Poland.

Czech Republic
In addition to the larger companies described above, the Czech Republic has some smaller piano brands too. Two examples are **Klima** and **Seidl**, the latter founded just a few years ago.

Other countries
There are piano manufacturers in many other countries too. One of the better-known examples is **Estonia**. This firm was founded in 1893 as the Tallinn Piano Factory in what is now the Estonian capital. Another is the high-end Italian make **Fazioli**, whose catalog includes the world's longest grand piano, the F 308 (10'2"). The uprights and grands of the German-sounding brands **Furstein** and **Schulze-Pollman** also come from Italy. Bechner and **Lippman** are two brands owned by a Dutch company; the instruments are made in the Ukraine. **Fritz Dobbert** pianos are made in Brazil.

GLOSSARY AND INDEX

This glossary contains short definitions of all the piano-related terms used in this book. There are also some words you won't find in the previous pages, but which you might well come across in magazines, catalogs, books, or Internet publications. The numbers refer to the pages where the terms are used in this book.

Acoustic piano The qualification 'acoustic' only became necessary after electric and (later) digital pianos had been invented – just like with guitars. In other words, an acoustic piano is an 'ordinary' piano.

Action *(7–9, 12, 44–49, 66–67, 104–105)* The mechanism that makes you play the instrument, consisting of dozens of wooden, felt, leather and metal parts per key.
The smallest upright pianos have an *indirect blow action* or *drop action*, which is mounted below the keys. Taller pianos have a *direct blow action*, as shown on page 8.

Agraffes *(58)* Brass string-guides.

Baby grand *(31)* A small grand piano.

Bach pedal See: *Sostenuto pedal.*

Back posts *(6–7, 40–41)* Wooden posts, reinforcing the structure of an upright piano. The posts in a grand piano are called *braces*.

Bass *(10–11, 52, 53, 55)* The lowest notes, produced by copper-wound strings.

Belly See: *Crown.*

Bird-cage action See: *Overdamper.*

Braces See: *Back posts.*

Bridge *(11, 57–58)* The bridges transmit the vibrations of the strings to the soundboard.

Capo bar, capo d'astro See: *Pressure bar.*

Caster cups *(18, 86–87)* Placed under a piano's casters to protect the floor, and sometimes to reduce sound transmission.

Casters *(36–37)* Piano wheels are called *casters.*

Celeste pedal See: *Practice pedal.*

Concert grand *(31)* The tallest grand piano.

Console *(30)* Small type of upright. See: *Spinet.*

Covered strings See: *Wound strings.*

Cross-strung *(12, 69)* By allowing the strings to run diagonally, so that the bass strings cross the other strings, longer strings can fit inside an equally large cabinet. Also called *over-strung.* Early pianos were *straight-strung.*

Crown *(60, 94)* The arch or *belly* of the soundboard.

Dampers *(8–9, 49–51)* Felt dampers mute the strings when you let go the keys.

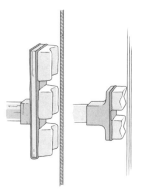

Large dampers for the bass strings, smaller ones for the higher-sounding strings.

Digital piano *(18–19, 82–83)* A piano without strings; the sounds are samples (digital recordings).

Direct blow action See: *Action.*

Down weight The force needed to play a soft note. See also: *Up weight.*

Duplex scale *(59)* A system which includes the far end of the higher treble strings in the sound production.

Escapement See: *Let-off.*

Equal temperament *(102–104)* Equal temperament tuning (a.k.a. *well-tempered scale*) allows pianos to be played in all key signatures.

Frame *(10, 114)* The cast-iron frame which, together with the back posts or braces, forms the backbone of an upright or grand piano. Also called the *plate*.

French polish *(32, 89)* Old-fashioned, expensive finish for pianos. The material used is *shellac*.

Front lid *(11, 39)* The front part of a grand piano lid.

Hammer heads, hammers *(5, 8, 49–52, 67, 94, 104–105)* Piano strings are struck with felt hammers.

Hybrid piano *(77)* An acoustic piano with a built-in digital piano module.

Indirect blow action See: *Action.*

Keyboard *(4, 37, 42–43, 82, 116)* Pianos usually have eighty-eight keys, although some older keyboards have eighty-five. See also: *Keys.*

Keys *(42–43, 90–91)* The keyboard usually has fifty-two ivory or synthetic-covered white keys (naturals) and thirty-six synthetic or wood black keys (sharps).

Let-off *(44, 45)* The let-off makes the hammer go back after hitting the string. Also

known as *escapement* or *set-off.*

MIDI *(80)* Using MIDI, you can hook up all kinds of electronic musical equipment (digital pianos, sound modules, synthesizers, and so on) to each other, or to computers.

Moderator stop See: *Practice pedal.*

Music desk *(5, 38)* Pianos always have a built-in music desk.

Mute pedal See: *Practice pedal.*

Naturals The white keys. The black keys are known as *sharps.*

Octave *(4, 13)* A piano keyboard has a good seven octaves.

Overdamper *(69)* Some (very) old uprights have the dampers above the hammers. Also called *birdcage action.*

Over-strung See: *Cross-strung.*

Pedals *(5–6, 12, 62–66)* Pianos have two or three pedals. The *sustain(ing)* or *damper pedal*, on the right, removes all the dampers from the strings. The left-hand pedal of an upright is the *soft pedal*; on a grand it's called the *una-corda pedal (65)*, reducing and altering the sound by slightly shifting the hammers. The middle pedal is usually a *practice pedal* or *mute pedal* on uprights *(63)*, activating a muffler, and a *sostenuto pedal (12, 66)* on grands. A sostenuto pedal makes only those notes already played sustain; it's also known as *Steinway pedal* or *Bach pedal*.

Pinblock *(10, 55, 69)* The tuning pins are set into a hardwood pinblock. Also called *wrest plank*.

Plate See: *Frame*.

Player piano *(109–110)* A piano that plays itself. The modern version works digitally, and can be used for recording too.

Practice pedal *(6, 63)* On uprights, the middle pedal is often used to lower a strip of felt between the hammers and the strings, muffling the overall volume for practicing purposes. The same system (also known as *celeste, moderator stop, muffler pedal* or *mute pedal*) is available in hand-operated versions as well.

Pressure bar *(58)* Strings are held in place either by a *pressure bar* (or *capo d'astro* or *capo bar*) or by *agraffes*. See also: *Agraffes*.

Regulating *(104–105)* The action of a piano needs periodic regulation in order to make the instrument play well and sound good.

Rim *(42)* The 'cabinet' of a grand piano.

Scale *(53–54)* Everything connected with the choice of strings is collectively called the scale, from the number of strings to their thickness, their length, their winding, and much more.

School piano *(36–37)* A piano with protective brackets, large wheels, and extra locks (see illustration on the next page).

Serial number *(69)* Necessary to determine an instrument's age.

Set-off See: *Let-off*.

Sharps *(42, 116)* The black keys. The white keys are known as *naturals*.

Shellac See: *French polish*.

Solid wood Most soundboards are made of planks

A school piano with locks, brackets and large wheels.

of solid spruce *(62, 114)*. Other parts (pin blocks, for instance) are virtually always laminated, made up of several plies of wood.

Sound module *(18, 77–81)* A box containing digital recordings (*samples*) of a piano or other instruments.

Soundboard *(6–7, 29, 30, 59, 60–62, 69, 93–94, 114)* The soul of a piano. The soundboard amplifies the sound of the strings.

Speaking length *(53–54)* The part of the string which vibrates, producing a note, when struck with a hammer. See also *Duplex scale*.

Spinet *(30, 46)* 1. Spinet piano. The very smallest

upright piano (up to some 40" or 100 cm high).
2. A historical keyboard instrument with plucked strings *(106)*.

Steinway pedal See: *Sostenuto pedal*.

Straight–strung See: *Cross-strung*.

Strings *(9, 29, 52–54, 68, 114–115)* A piano has around two hundred and twenty steel strings. Only the lowest bass notes have one string each.
The upper bass notes have two strings each: the double or two-string *unisons (9–10, 53)*. From the first low treble notes upwards there are three strings per note: the three-string unisons *(9, 54)*.

Studio piano *(30)* Medium to full-size upright piano.

Sustain pedal, Sustaining pedal See: *Pedals.*

Tenor See: *Treble.*

Treble *(10, 52, 53, 75)* The highest five octaves (approximately) of a piano, sometimes divided into *low treble* or *tenor* and *high treble*, the latter referring to the highest three octaves.

Tuning *(25, 68, 99–104).*

Tuning pins *(10, 55–58, 69)* Steel pins used to tune the strings. Also called *wrest pins.*

Una-corda pedal See: *Pedals*

Unison See: *Strings.*

Up weight *(46)* The force with which a key comes back up.

Vertical piano Another name for upright piano.

Voicing *(51, 104–105, 116)* Treating the hammer heads to adjust or improve the tone of the instrument.

Well-tempered scale See: *Equal temperament.*

Wheels See: *Casters.*

Wound strings *(9, 53)* The bass strings are wound with copper wire, the extra mass allowing them to sound low enough without becoming too long.

Wrest pins See: *Tuning pins.*

Wrest plank See: *Pinblock.*

TIPCODE LIST

The Tipcodes in this book offer easy access to short movies, photo series, soundtracks, and other additional information at www.tipbook.com. For your convenience, the Tipcodes in Tipbook Piano have been listed below.

Tipcode	Topic	Chapters	Pages
PIANO-001	Various styles of music	**1**	1
PIANO-002	An octave; eight white keys	**2**	4
PIANO-003	Practice pedal	**2, 3, 5**	6, 17, 63
PIANO-004	Upright action	**2**	8
PIANO-005	Grand action	**2**	12
PIANO-006	Una-corda pedal	**2, 5**	12, 65
PIANO-007	Sostenuto pedal	**2, 5**	12, 66
PIANO-008	The range of a piano	**2**	13
PIANO-009	Let-off or escapement	**5**	44
PIANO-010	Dampers; no dampers	**5**	50
PIANO-011	Sustain pedal	**5**	62
PIANO-012	Hybrid piano's mute rail	**5, 7**	64, 77
PIANO-013	Tuning fork	**5**	68
PIANO-014	Three test chords	**6**	73
PIANO-015	One test chord	**6**	73
PIANO-016	Various sounds	**7**	78
PIANO-017	Effects	**7**	79
PIANO-018	Meantone tuning and equal temperament	**10**	104
PIANO-019	Inside a piano factory	**13**	114

WANT TO KNOW MORE?

Tipbooks give you basic information on the instrument of your choice and everything connected with it. Of course, there's a lot more to be found on all the subjects you came across on the previous pages. A selection of magazines, books, and websites, as well as some background on the makers of the Tipbook series.

MAGAZINES
The following magazines may be of interest for pianists:
- *Piano Today*, phone (914) 244 8500, www.pianotoday.com.
- *The Piano Technicians Journal* is a technical publication of the Piano Technicians Guild (see below).
- *International Piano* (UK), phone +44 141 30277 43, www.pianomagazine.com (international subscriptions possible).
- *Keyboard Companion*, www.keyboardcompanion.com.

Other magazines
The magazines *Piano & Keyboard* and *Clavier* did not seem to be available when this book was printed.

BOOKS
There are dozens of books on pianos, ranging from publications on the history and workings of the instrument to photo books and extensive descriptions of the way they are built. A very limited selection is given below.
- *The Piano Book – Buying & Owing a New or Used Piano*, Larry Fine (Brookside Press, 2001, fourth edition; 244 pages; ISBN 1 929 14501 2; also available in hardcover).

An annual supplement describes all changes in the piano market and lists prices for every brand and model of new piano on the market (over 2,500 of them), plus advice on how to estimate actual selling prices (see www.pianobook.com for more information).

- *Piano – Evolution, Design and Performance*, David Crombie (Balafon, 1995; 112 pages; ISBN 1 871547 99 7).
- *Piano Servicing, Tuning and Rebuilding*, For the Professional, the Student, the Hobbyist, by Arthur A. Reblitz (Vestal Press Ltd., 1996; 327 pages; ISBN 1 879 51103 7).
- *The Cambridge Companion to the Piano*, by Davis Rowland (Cambridge University Press, 2000; 325 pages; ISBN 0 521 47986 X).
- *Piano Roles – Three Hundred Years of Life with the Piano*, by James Parakilas (Yale University Press, 2000; 461 pages; ISBN 0 300 08055 7).
- *Giraffes, Black Dragons, and Other Pianos: A Technological History from Cristofori to the Modern Concert Grand*, by Edwin M. Good (Stanford University Press, 2001; 312 pages; ISBN 0 804 73316 3).

INTERNET

Internet addresses tend to change fast, but with a bit of luck some of the following sites will give you a good starting point and countless links to other sites. You may also find a teacher or a tuner via these sites or the others mentioned elsewhere in this section.

- The Piano Education Page (www.unm.edu/~loritaf/pnoedmn.html).
- The Piano Home Page (www.serve.com/marbeth/piano.html).
- The Piano Page (www.ptg.org): site of the Piano Technicians Guild.
- The UK Piano Page (www.uk-piano.org).
- Piano World (www.pianoworld.com).

PIANO TECHNICIANS AND TUNERS

You can find a certified piano technician through the following organizations:

- USA and Canada: Piano Technicians Guild (PTG), ptg@ptg.org, www.ptg.org.
- USA, Canada, and international: Master Piano

Technicians of America, info@masterpianotechnicians.
org; www.masterpianotechnicians.org.
· Canada: Canadian Association of Piano Technicians
(CAPT), www.telusplanet.net/public/atonal/capt.
Ontario Guild of Piano Technicians,
www.nebula.on.ca/ogpt.
· Australia and New Zealand: Australasian Piano Tuners
and Technicians Association (APTTA), fax +61 (0)2
9351 1200, sec@aptta.org.au, www.aptta.org.au.
· For other countries, additional information and updated details, please check the website of the Piano
Technicians Guild (see above).

OTHER BOOKS IN THIS SERIES

*This book is part of a fast-growing series. In Tipbook Music
On Paper – Basic Theory* you'll find everything on dynamic
markings, repeat signs, octave symbols, and all the rest you
need to know to read sheet music, plus a clear explanation
of basic music theory. You'll also find lots of easy-to-play
examples. Things like writing music notation, scales, and
intervals are also covered. An extensive index makes this
book an ideal reference work. *Tipbook Keyboard and Digital
Piano* has countless tips on buying these instruments and
explanations of all the technical terms.

ABOUT THE MAKERS

Journalist, writer, and musician Hugo Pinksterboer,
(co)author of the Tipbook Series, has published hundreds
of interviews, articles, and instrument, video, CD, and book
reviews for national and international music magazines.
He wrote the reference work for cymbals (*The Cymbal
Book*) and has written and developed a wide variety of
manuals and courses, both for musicians and non-
musicians.

Illustrator, designer, and musician Gijs Bierenbroodspot
has worked as an art director for a wide variety of
magazines, and has developed numerous ad campaigns.
While searching for information about saxophone
mouthpieces, he got the idea for this series of books on
music and musical instruments – and has created the
layout and the illustrations for them as well. He has also
found a good mouthpiece, by the way.

ESSENTIAL DATA

If you want to sell your instrument, if something happens to it or it needs repairing, it's always helpful to have all the relevant data at hand. Here are two pages to make those notes. You can also list when your piano is due for another tuning, and any questions you want to ask your piano technician – from sticking keys when it's damp to rattles and buzzes you only hear in the winter.

INSURANCE

Company:	
Phone:	Fax:
Agent:	
Phone:	Fax:
Policy number:	
Premium:	

INSTRUMENT DETAILS

Make and type:	
Serial number:	
Price:	
Color/model:	
Date of purchase:	
Place of purchase:	
Phone:	Fax:

TUNER/TECHNICIAN

Name:	
Address:	
Phone:	Fax:
E-mail:	

TUNINGS

Date of last/next tuning   Remarks

_____

_____

_____

_____

_____

_____

_____

_____

_____

_____

_____

_____

_____

QUESTIONS FOR THE TUNER/TECHNICIAN

....

....

....

....

....

....

....

....

....

....

....

....

....

....

....

....

ADDITIONAL NOTES

TIPBOOK SERIES
MUSIC AND MUSICAL INSTRUMENTS*
Released
Tipbook Acoustic Guitar
Tipbook Clarinet
Tipbook Drums
Tipbook Piano
Tipbook Trumpet & Trombone
Tipbook Violin & Viola

Expected in 2002
Tipbook Electric Guitar and Bass Guitar
Tipbook Flute
Tipbook Home Keyboard and Digital Piano
Tipbook Music on Paper – Basic Theory
Tipbook Saxophone
Tipbook Vocals

TBA
Tipbook Accordion
Tipbook Amplifiers and Effects
Tipbook Background Brass
Tipbook Cello
Tipbook Composing and Arranging
Tipbook Home Recording
Tipbook Improvisation
Tipbook MIDI
Tipbook Music for Children
Tipbook Music on Paper part II
Tipbook Oboe and Bassoon
Tipbook Percussion
Tipbook Synthesizer and Sampler

*Titles subject to change.

Want to know what's available today?
Take a look at www.tipbook.com.